Search For Oli's Gold

Danger, adversity, and betrayal lie in wait on the 19th century frontier.

Book Two

James Oliver Virmala

Edition 2

ISBN-13: 978-0-9972536-1-0

DEDICATION

This book is dedicated to Mark who has assisted
me in bringing these books to you.

.

CONTENTS

Chapter 1   Pg 1

Chapter 2   Pg 9

Chapter 3   Pg 20

Chapter 4   Pg 35

Chapter 5   Pg 49

Chapter 6   Pg 69

Chapter 7   Pg 88

Chapter 8   Pg 101

Chapter 9   Pg 127

Chapter 10   Pg 157

Chapter 11   Pg 167

Chapter 12   Pg 173

Chapter 13   Pg 194

Chapter 14   Pg 219

Chapter 15   Pg 233

More Gold   Pg 252

Other Books By The Author   Pg 254

ACKNOWLEDGMENTS

I would like to thank Randy and Mary for the picture used on the cover of this book.

Thanks to Mark who edits my books. I appreciate his historical knowledge which keeps me thinking and writing in the period of the book.

Thanks to the many friends who read the books. Even more important, sharing their favorite parts of the books which is priceless to me.

CHAPTER 1

The bright midday sun brought the promise of spring. The mood of the small group, standing around a freshly filled grave, was in stark contrast to the warm surroundings. It was early April 1866 and Joan August wept softly at her husband Oli's grave. She was comforted by her two sons and daughter. The supportive crowd from the town of Elkader, Iowa had returned home. All around trees were budding out, crocus and daffodils were in bloom, and robins were busy building nests. The beauty of spring was lost on them.

Leaving the grave, they slowly walked to the carriage. Karl, the eldest son, helped his mother, Joan, into the seat. The other two children, Tony and Jenny, decided to walk. They watched as Karl drove the carriage back toward their home overlooking Turkey River.

Jenny and Tony went to the house. Karl was unhitching the horses and putting them into the corral behind the barn. He was 21. Karl had his father's broad shoulders and narrow hips. Today his blond hair was matted to his forehead, and there was sadness in his blue eyes.

Oli and Joan had built their home just above the spot where they had first met. The grassy slope running down from the house was where Joan had been standing when Oli had emerged from the river in tattered clothes, 26 years earlier.

The buildings showed weathering, but were well-built. The two-story house was constructed from hand-hewed logs fitted tightly and chinked. The floors were broad oak planks sanded smooth. A full-length porch ran along the river side of the house. The first floor had a large kitchen and living area. A bedroom and pantry were off to one side. The second floor had two bedrooms, one for Jenny and the other for the two boys.

The living area had a field stone fireplace, but the cooking and most of the heating were provided by the cast iron kitchen stove. The house was kept spotless by Joan and Jenny.

Several family friends were at the house and had brought food. Jenny joined her fiancé, Albert Keller, on the porch swing. She was 19. Her blond hair had red highlights. There was a sprinkle of freckles across her cheeks and she had her mother's hazel eyes. Albert looked up and smiled. He was the sheriff's son, and had a good job at the saw mill. He and Jenny were planning a June wedding.

Tony was the youngest, just 16. He had wavy brown hair and green eyes. He settled his thin, wiry frame into the cowhide chair his father had used and looked at the fireplace. Only a couple hours ago, his father's coffin had been placed in front of it before being moved to the church for services. The house felt empty without the sound of his father's laughter.

He couldn't believe that just two days before the family had been sitting around the dinner table, laughing and talking. Shouts of, "Fire!" had brought them rushing out of the house. They were greeted by smoke and flames coming from their neighbor's house. Mrs. Adams had stood in front and cried for help. Her daughter Lizzy had been in bed on the second floor with the flu, trapped by the flames.

His father, Oli August, had not hesitated. He'd grabbed a ladder and climbed up to the second story window to find her. He had appeared at the window with the child in his arms. A loud crash was the only warning as the roof had caved in. In desperation, he had tossed the child to the outstretched arms of Sheriff Keller.

Before he'd had a chance to exit the window, the wall had collapsed, sending sparks and flames into the evening sky. It took only moments for his sons Karl and Tony to pull him from the burning timbers, but it had been too late. At the age of 51, Oli August died as he'd lived, helping others.

Karl found himself drawn to the shop next to the house. It was where his father had earned a living. The weathered sign read:

Oli's Repair Shop
No Job Too Small
Some Too Big

The shop building had been the first home that Oli and Joan had lived in. The two-room building had been converted into Oli's shop after the log home was built.

Karl knew that he should be in the house with everyone else, but he needed time to grieve alone. He tried to be the strong one, now that he was the man of the house, and had to keep up a front for everyone else. He sat in the quiet of his father's shop and wept. Just a few months ago, he had returned home after the Civil War ended.

He had been with the 3rd Iowa Light Artillery. Karl had joined when he was 17. His first action had been at The Battle of Pea Ridge, in Arkansas, in 1862. Karl had continued seeing action for the rest of the war until the being mustered out in October 1865.

He had returned to find that most of his friends were married and starting families. His father's unexpected death left Karl questioning the time he'd spent away in the Army. He now felt cheated out of the last four years with his father, but did not regret fighting for the Union. It had been a good cause for the freedom of all men.

Looking around the shop, he saw the shelves neatly stacked with items used for repairs. Other shelves had items that had been left for repair. They would have to be returned to their owners without being fixed.

One shelf had four small wooden boxes. Each contained flint, tinder, and striking steel. Their father had put them together and always carried at least two when he traveled. He had even found a local man to teach them how to make fire rubbing sticks together. Tony would kid his father and ask him why he didn't just carry matches.

Karl smiled as he remembered his father's response: "When you are out in the wild with those wet matches eating raw meat, I'll be sitting next to a nice fire roasting a prairie chicken."

The boys never fully appreciated their father's need to be able to make fire, even after he told them the stories of being without it in the wilderness.

Oli had spent many hours teaching the boys and Jenny how to survive in the woods. He would take them to a remote camping area and make them lead him back out. Often, they went out on a fishing trip without a tent or ground cloth and had to build a shelter when they got there.

Hours were spent throwing a knife against a board leaning on the side of the shop. Their father would tell them stories of Wink, the man who had modified the knife that Oli dubbed the Good Knife, and the man who had taught him how to throw. He had never let them use the Good Knife for practice.

Karl could hold his own throwing, but Tony was the best with a knife. Jenny had practiced with them when she was young, but their mother hadn't felt it was right for a lady as she got older.

The longest trip Karl had taken with his father had been at the age of 12. His father had built a 19-ft canoe. It'd been midsummer when they had pushed off toward the Mississippi River. Their mother and the two younger children had stood on the bank of Turkey River and waved goodbye. Karl had continued to look back and wave until they were out of sight.

"If you have waved enough, it is time to grab a paddle, son," his father had said.

Karl had always been older than his years and had done his share of paddling. He'd noticed a rectangular package in the middle of the boat, under their packs. He'd asked his father what it was. His father had said that it was ballast to keep the boat upright.

Satisfied with the explanation, Karl had been fascinated looking at the river. They'd spent nights along the shore, cooking fish or other game they had gotten. They had caught a steamboat in Dubuque at the landing next to Catfish Creek. The canoe had been loaded onto the steamboat. Upon leaving the steamboat, the canoe had been used as they'd gone up the Ohio River.

One afternoon, they'd come upon an old landing. It'd had a few buildings with roofs sagging. One had had a long bar on one side, another building had smelled of cow manure. Karl had watched his father's face as he looked around. While Karl had seen an abandoned landing, he'd seen that his father saw something altogether different.

"You can almost hear the piano," his father had said as they'd walked back to the water.

Four days later, they had pulled into a secluded cove. They had stopped in many before, but his father would say, "It's the wrong one," and they would move on.

Karl had watched his father walk around the small clearing. There had been evidence of several fires. Stopping and kneeling next to some stones, his father had smiled. "This is it, Karl. This is Isaac's grave."

He'd showed Karl some scattered stones, with one stone that had a small cross chipped into it. Moving back to the canoe, Karl had helped his father carry the rectangular package to the grave. Removing the canvas wrap, Karl had seen the headstone.

Isaac Franklin
1839
A Mountain Man

They'd taken care in placing the headstone. His father had said that they did not want the next flood to take it away.

That night, Karl had sat next to the fire roasting some fish while his father spent some quiet time at the grave. He'd then come back to the fire and told Karl the story of the trip down the Ohio River when he'd come west. Karl was spellbound during the story, with visions of his father standing in the boat, fighting off attacking Indians.

Karl had asked his father, "What happened at the landing?"

His father had smiled and sat back. "I fixed the boat."

Karl remembered the excitement when they'd returned from the trip, telling his sister and brother about the adventure and an embellished version of their father's trip down the Ohio River.

When Oli had met Joan on the banks of Turkey River, the town was called Pony Hollow. In 1847, it had been renamed Elkader, after an Algerian hero. The town was growing slowly. It had a newspaper, a newly rebuilt gristmill, and even exported some flour to Europe.

Oli had been well-liked by the town's people. That is, except the Wolfe brothers. Jake and Tate Wolfe had a successful trading business. Tate had wanted to court Joan and she had chosen Oli over him. Jake's wrist had been broken at their first meeting and it had never healed correctly. Their eldest boy had often fought with Karl and Tony. It had given Oli's boys a chance to hone their fighting skills.

CHAPTER 2

The days following the funeral were busy for Karl and Tony. Items from their father's shop had to be returned to the owners. Any that the boys could fix were repaired, and the money paid went to their mother. The rest were returned, as received, with apologies.

Josh Wolfe was the youngest of Tate's boys. He was short in stature, and skinny. He had a wild shock of sandy brown hair. Despite the friction between their fathers, Josh was a friend of Tony. He came by and asked if there was anything he could do to help.

Karl watched Tony and Josh head toward the barn to take care of the stock. Jenny found Karl cleaning up after a project in the shop.

"I am worried about mother," she said.

Karl hung the broom on its pegs and turned to his sister. "What are you talking about?"

Brushing a loose strand of hair off her face, she continued. "Jacob Wolfe stopped by this morning. After he left, mother sat for the longest time staring out the window. She then went to her room. I went in and she was sitting on the bed, holding father's money belt. Karl, her eyes were filled with tears."

Karl frowned. "Maybe she was thinking about father and just got down. It may be nothing more than that."

"I don't think so. The look on her face was . . . it scared me, Karl." Jenny began to cry.

Putting his arm around her shoulder, Karl said, "Jenny, after supper tonight we will talk to mother. If something other than losing father is bothering her, we will try and find out."

Supper was a quiet affair. Jenny kept looking at Karl and motioning toward their mother. If Tony noticed anything, he made no indication of it. With the dishes cleared, the four of them sat down with cups of coffee.

Just as Karl got the courage to try and find out what was on their mother's mind, she looked up and said, "We have a problem. If you recall, when the tornado damaged Gunter Hahn's hotel, your father helped him get on his feet again. We used our home and buildings as collateral to secure a loan so he could rebuild."

"By the time his hotel was repaired and back in business, another hotel funded by the Wolfe brothers opened. It has cut his business in less than half, and he hasn't the money to pay the loan. The Wolfe brothers have taken over the note on our property from the bank. The note becomes due in eight months. If not paid in full, they will own our home."

The three children stared at their mother with disbelief on their faces. Tony growled, "They can't do that. They have to take the hotel!"

Shaking her head, their mother said, "The hotel is of no value to them. Our property is, and that is what's on the note. I understand from Mrs. Adams that they bought her property after the fire. They want to expand their trading company along the river. The Adams property is too small to do this, but with ours, it will be plenty."

Karl pounded his fist on the table. "They will take our property over my dead body! I am going to find Jacob Wolfe and shove the note down his throat."

Jenny's eyes were large as she looked at her mother. Joan continued. "No, Karl that is not how things should be done. How do you think your sister would feel if her fiancé's father had to come here and arrest you? Jacob Wolfe is within his rights."

Moving over and leaning against the fireplace, Karl asked, "How much is the note, mother?"

Joan set her cup down and smoothed her apron. "We owe just under $10,000. Your father and I had some money set aside, but it's not near enough to cover that."

Karl and Tony sat on the front porch, digesting what their mother had told them. They heard someone coming around the house. Albert Keller came to take Jenny to a friend's party.

"Good evening, Albert," Tony said.

Karl invited Albert to sit. "Jenny is a bit behind tonight. We were a little slow finishing supper."

Albert sat down and handed Karl a newspaper. "I just finished reading it and thought you might like it. There is a great article on cattle in Texas."

Albert had always dreamed of being a cowboy. He had intended to go south until he met Jenny. A pretty girl had a way of changing a man's plans. The three of them made small talk until Jenny was ready.

Karl watched them walk away. "He is a very lucky man, Tony. His father helped him get a job in the office of the gristmill, and he is set to marry our sister."

Tony shook his head. "I wouldn't want to work in an office. I would want to have some adventures first."

"Remember father's adventure, Tony. It left him cold and hungry for many months. Not to mention almost losing his life in the process."

Tony stood and looked at the river. "I think it would be worth it, just for the excitement."

Karl looked at his brother. Tony had been too young to join when Karl had enlisted in the army. He had tried to keep his letters upbeat when he'd written home. Maybe he'd made army life sound too much like an adventure.

And then there had been the stories their father had told about being on the wagon train and spending the winter in a cabin with only the body of Don Sikes to talk to. Karl admitted that it would give one the yen to roam. At 16, Tony was just becoming a man and had a great desire to strike out on his own.

Karl had seen death and destruction during the war. Too many men died in battle, and as many from disease. He had felt the loneliness of being away from family. These feelings could not be explained to the young. They had to be experienced.

He sat up late, reading the newspaper Albert had brought. The article on Texas cattle made him start thinking. The article spoke of maverick cattle. They were unbranded cattle, running loose for the taking. In Texas, the cattle were worth nothing. If they could be driven to Kansas they were worth as much as $20 each. Just 500 cattle could pay off the note.

Karl slept restlessly that night. He kept thinking about a cattle drive. While in the army he had been assigned to a group that had raided and driven 1,000 cattle to feed the Union troops. He'd learned much from the drive. He understood the dangers and difficulties of handling a large herd. Of course, they would not have Confederates shooting at them, but there would be Indians and herd cutters.

It would require money to undertake the venture. Food would have to be purchased. Each man would need up to five horses. Equipment such as a chuck wagon would be needed, not to mention a cook. They would need enough cattle to make up for losses along the drive. The sun was only a couple hours from rising when he finally fell asleep.

After a breakfast of pancakes with sweet maple syrup and plenty of butter, Karl sat on the porch drinking coffee and waiting for his mother to finish in the kitchen. He could hear her working the pump at the sink.

Not every house had a hand pump right in the kitchen. It saved carrying water from the river or a well. His father had worked very hard to give their mother every possible comfort. Joan came out and looked at Karl.

"Could you bring some wood in for me? I have to do some wash this morning."

"Yes, mother. Sit for a minute, though. I have something I want to talk to you about."

He quickly told her about the cattle in Texas and the possibility of putting a herd together. While she thought about what he had said, Karl hurried to the woodshed and returned with a large armload of wood. Having been asked to help, Tony followed with another armload.

Brushing the wood chips from their clothes, the two sat next to their mother. Karl continued to explain a plan that he had worked out. Glancing at his brother, he knew that there was no turning back. Tony's green eyes were fairly dancing with excitement.

Joan got up and looked at the boys. "I need to do some wash. I think best when I am busy. We can talk about his later."

She walked into the house with a knot in her stomach. Why do men always want to go on adventures? Oli had wanted to go back and find more gold to pay off the note. The Indians were active in the Dakotas, and she hadn't let him do so.

She knew as she scrubbed the clothes on the washboard that no matter what she said, they would go. She just had to figure how it could be done with the least risk. When Karl was in the war she had prayed every day for his safe return. With Oli gone, she didn't think that she could bear to lose one or both of her sons. When Karl and Tony came over to help her hang clothes on the line, she knew that there was no putting off an answer.

One would have thought that the circus was coming to town by the excitement that the two men displayed. They were busy making plans and looking over every map they could find. The Chisholm Trail was the best route to drive the cattle.

Karl had saved some money during the war. They made discreet inquiries about earning some additional money. They would need $2,000 to fund the venture. Karl was feeding the stock when Tony came by with the milk bucket.

"Karl, don't be mad at me."

Karl looked over at his brother. Setting the pitchfork down, Karl spoke in the calmest voice he could muster. "Don't be mad about what?"

"Josh wants to come with us."

Feeling a slow burn, Karl said, "How does Josh know about our plan?"

"We were sharing some of his father's rye and I slipped up," Tony said sheepishly.

Picking up the pitchfork, Karl continued to feed the stock. Only now he had a death grip on the fork.

"Karl, I know you are mad at me, but just maybe there is something to be gained. Josh said they need to move some horses to Fort Dakota. His father is having a hard time finding someone to do it. He is offering $500. Maybe the three of us can earn money for the cattle drive."

Karl shook his head. He could not help but wonder, was nothing simple? "Fort Dakota is through Indian territory, Tony. We will lose two to three weeks moving the horses. It is time we cannot afford."

Tony set his jaw firm. It reminded Karl of his father when he disagreed with his mother. "Karl, we need to raise money. We will need horses. All of that will take time. Maybe the moving of the horses will be a good use of our time. Let's at least talk to Josh's father. We don't have to tell him about the cattle drive."

Karl and Tony sat on straight back chairs waiting to talk to Tate Wolfe. The air was stale with the smell of old carpet. A skinny, hook-nosed clerk sat behind a desk and instructed them to wait. He seemed to take pleasure in their uncomfortable chairs.

The boys were just about to give up when Tate stepped out, filling the doorway of his office. "Come on in and state your business."

While his tone was not demeaning, it had a hint of impatience to it. Pointing to two straight back chairs in front of his desk, Tate said, "Have a seat. I don't have much time. I wouldn't even have seen you, except Josh asked me to."

Karl found that the legs of these chairs were shorter and they were looking up at the big man. Karl now knew that Tate was aware of their plans, including the cattle drive.

"We would like to talk to you about driving horses to Fort Dakota . . ."

Cutting him off with a wave of his hand, Tate interrupted. "I know about your grand plan to drive cattle to pay off the note. Frankly, I do not care about that. I need horses driven to Fort Dakota. If you are interested in doing this for $500, then we can move ahead. Only thing I require is you take Josh along to watch over my interest."

Karl tried to respond, but Tate Wolfe talked over him. "I will also make some horses available for the cattle drive if you include my older son, James. Now, I don't have much time to have you thinking about this. James will meet you in St Louis after you drop the horses off. You can catch a steamboat down the Missouri."

In frustration, Karl stood up. "We will need the money in advance. James and Josh will get paid $30 a month once we start rounding up cattle. We would want the extra horses waiting in Texas. It would take too much time to drive the horses from Fort Dakota to Texas."

Karl felt the hair on his neck bristling, and it took all of his composure not to tell Tate to forget it. Tate Wolfe stuck a fat cigar into his mouth and took a long drag.

"Josh will pay you the $500 from the proceeds of the sale of the horses. You will start with 50 horses. We split the cost of any losses. Other than that, the deal sounds okay to me. I'll have my lawyer write up a contract."

Karl was steaming. He knew that he needed to control his temper. "You have a contract written up, but make sure a schoolboy can understand it."

Karl was surprised when he saw that the contract was short and to the point, with no clever language that could leave anything to doubt. There was only one explanation: Tate Wolfe was sure that the venture would fail and that the property would fall nicely into his hands.

Josh was not a problem, but James could be trouble. Karl couldn't count the number of times that they had fought. James was bigger when they'd been young, and would always win. Karl had shot up in his teens and won his share.

Unlike Josh, who had a slight build, James was medium height and stocky. His hair was darker than his brother's. He had a thick, bushy moustache and a receding hair line. He liked to squeeze his victims when he fought, and when they weakened James would raise them over his head and throw them.

Fortunately, he had not perfected that method of fighting the last time that he and Karl had met. It was said that he'd killed a man fighting in Dubuque. It had been considered a fair fight, so he'd not been arrested.

CHAPTER 3

It was late April when they moved the horses out. They would get $50 each when delivered at the fort. The ground would be fairly open, so they figured that Karl, Tony, and Josh should be able to control them with few losses.

Once Albert had found out about the cattle drive, he'd convinced Jenny to postpone the wedding. He'd insisted on going along, knowing that it would be the only chance to live his dream. He would be going down with James Wolfe to meet them in St. Louis. They planned to leave two weeks after the horses moved out.

Joan sat with her oldest son the night before they left. "Promise me you will take care of Tony. He is young and may take unnecessary chances."

Karl took his mother's hand. "Don't worry mother, Tony is a smart boy. We have a good plan. Albert will be with us, along with the Wolfe boys. We will hire a couple more in Texas. We should be back here with the money before the leaves change."

Joan went to the bedroom and returned with a small, leather-bound book. Setting it on the table in front of Karl, she looked into his wise blue eyes.

"This was your father's ledger. You will need a tally book for the cattle. I want you to take it with you. I put in a new pencil for you."

Karl picked up the polished leather-bound ledger. He had seen it many times, but had never been allowed to look through or handle it. Karl's mother continued to talk softly with him late into the night. She knew that the boys were leaving the next morning and dreaded it.

The morning they left was gray, with a fine mist. The horses looked rough, with half of their winter coat shed.

Tony looked at his brother Karl and was very proud. Karl looked every bit the cowboy, sitting tall in the saddle, wearing a dark gray wool shirt and canvas pants. He had medium heel cowboy boots and a sheepskin vest.

Karl had a Colt Army Model 1860 ball and cap revolver on one hip and a knife on the other. He had a Henry .44 caliber rimfire repeating rifle in the scabbard on the horse. He'd brought these guns home, along with an extra rifle, from the war. He unrolled his rain slicker to keep dry.

Tony had a second Henry rifle brought back by Karl. His revolver was an 1851 Navy Colt. Sheriff

Keller had given them a good deal on the gun. It had been taken off a prisoner who'd later escaped.

Being the best at throwing a knife, Tony had been given the Good Knife by his father. He wore it down the nape of his neck, the same way Oli had.

Josh had an Army Colt and a Sharps rifle given to him by his father, Tate Wolfe.

They all had flat-brimmed hats with round crowns that had been purchased from the mercantile.

The horses had been driven recently and took to the trail without much problem. Taking advantage of a cool rain, they ran the horses for the first couple miles. They then settled down to a walk.

The fort was about 300 miles from Elkader, and if they could make 18 miles per day the trip would take just under three weeks.

Karl was riding a black gelding with a smooth, mile-eating gait. Tony rode a chestnut horse with a white blaze on its nose. Josh rode a bay. All had bedrolls and saddlebags. The first two days it rained off and on. The nights were damp and uncomfortable. Their meals consisted of jerky, biscuits, and hot coffee.

A large sorrel mare took the lead of the horses and seemed content to head west. One of the men rode on each flank of the horses, and one rode drag. The wet ground kept the dust down, so even riding drag wasn't a bad position.

The spring grass was plentiful and Karl would look for a place for the stock to graze each night.

Five days into their trip they passed a low log building. Someone had built a trading post next to a stream.

It was a good chance to replenish some supplies, so they circled the horses and moved them onto some grass after they watered in the stream. Josh offered to stay with the horses while Karl and Tony went to get supplies.

Stepping into the building, Karl and Tony hesitated while their eyes grew accustomed to the low light. There was a plank bar along one side that also served as a sales counter. Furs were stacked up in one corner, and shelves of goods were on the walls. There was a potbelly stove in the middle of the room with a coffee pot. Some barrels of goods and coils of rope were in another corner.

Karl and Tony stepped up to the bar and each had a shot of rye to toast the trip. Karl looked at a large bearskin hanging on the wall behind the bar.

"Nice looking bearskin."

The old proprietor gave Karl a big toothless smile. His thin greasy hair was plastered to his scalp. "I shot it several years ago. I would have sold it, but the right side is damaged." He showed Karl a large scarred area.

Karl and Tony looked at each other. "It couldn't be," Tony said to Karl.

"Where did you shoot the bear?" Karl asked.

"It was up the stream a way, couple of miles. There is a stone ledge and a cave. I think it was wintering in the cave," the old man replied as he wiped his nose with the same rag that he was polishing glasses with.

"Another drink, boys?" Shaking their heads, Karl and Tony moved over to the shelves and started picking out a few things they could use.

Chuckling, Karl and Tony left the trading post. "I was going to ask about some coffee, but wasn't sure how he cleaned the cups," Tony said.

Swinging into the saddle, Karl grinned. "Let's ride and see if we can find the cave."

Turning their horses upstream, they rode, searching for the ledge and cave. Oli had told the boys stories of sharing the cave with the injured bear while wandering through the wilderness. They figured that the damaged hide in the trading post might have come from that very bear.

Spotting a stone ledge, a cave was found behind tag alders growing next to the ledge. Tony dismounted and looked into the dark opening. Karl looked up the down the stream. This could be the same place where his father had gone through a forest fire and had taken refuge in a cave occupied by a bear.

Tony crawled back out of the cave, brushing dust from his cloths. "It is big enough to hold the bear and father." Karl felt a chill, realizing that might be the same ground his father had been on so many years ago.

They returned to the camp just after sundown with stories to share with Josh. Josh had the fire going, and a pot of beans with side meat bubbling. Tony rode out to check on the horses, while Karl stowed the new supplies between the saddlebags.

Josh looked at Karl. "Your father always treated me well. Even though he did not get along with my father, he treated me as an individual. I miss him, Karl."

Karl looked into the dark, toward the horses. "We all do, Josh, we all do."

Karl remembered how his father had treated people. He'd considered everyone a friend unless they proved otherwise. He'd been willing to help those in need. Often, he would fix things at no charge for a family that could not afford to pay. Nothing was ever said. Even those without money needed things fixed, and he'd been able to help.

He remembered a family his father had helped. They'd had little money and had needed a roof on their house. When they'd sold their place, the man had come to see Oli before they'd left. He had the money he'd owed. His father had refused to take it. He'd told them that they might need it during the trip. When they got to the other end, send it to him if they had it. If they didn't, don't worry about it. About a month later, his father had received a letter with the money.

Josh turned out to be good on the trail. He did his share driving the horses, and more than his share in camp. Josh liked cooking over a fire. Karl and Tony were only too happy to let him. Each took care of their own dishes, and they all pitched in cleaning up the cook pots.

One afternoon, Tony pointed at some deer browsing in a clearing. He pulled away from the herd, left his horse tied to some brush, then silently stalked the deer. At about 60 paces away, he brought up the Henry rifle and drew a bead on a young buck. He squeezed the shot off and the deer leaped into the air and collapsed. The others bounded off into a valley.

They all enjoyed broiled venison steaks that night. Josh saved the liver for breakfast. He planned to make a hearty breakfast of liver and fried potatoes. Some of the extra venison would be broiled and eaten cold with biscuits for the midday meal.

The wooded area was fading away and they were crossing rolling prairie. It did not make sense to be too conspicuous, so they kept to the valleys. The grass was good and water plentiful. Other than the first couple days of rain, the weather was dry, with cool mornings and comfortable sunny days.

Karl was bunching some stragglers that wanted to eat rather than walk, when he heard Josh shout, "Indians, we got Indians up ahead!"

The horses were more than willing to stop and graze, once they weren't being pushed. Karl and Tony joined Josh in front of the herd. There were ten Indians spread out in front of them.

Karl's first thought was to run the herd through them and keep going. Shaking that idea away, he realized that it was exactly what they wanted to happen. They wanted the herd running and scattered. They could then drive a number of the horses away.

Karl turned to the others. "Tony, you and I will go up to them. Maybe we can make a deal. Josh, you stay with the herd. If something happens to Tony or me, get the horses running and you go the other way. I am sure it is the horses they want, and you should be able to escape."

Josh complained about being left, but Karl was firm with his instructions. As he and Tony rode toward the Indians, they carried rifles across the front of their saddles.

Karl spoke softly to Tony. "If this goes sour, you turn your horse and don't stop running until you get back to Elkader. Mother would never forgive me if I let something happen to you."

Staring straight ahead, Tony replied, "It ain't going to happen, Karl. If mother knew I left you alone to fight these Indians, I would spend the rest of my days sleeping in the barn. We're brothers, and we will stand together, or fall together."

Karl was shocked by his brother's answer. He had always looked upon Tony as a youngster who needed protecting, but he was sitting tall, ready to do a man's work today.

The Indians closed in a bit on both sides as the brothers approached the apparent leader seated on a brown and white pinto. Stopping a short distance away, Karl turned his horse just a bit to bring the barrel of his rifle to bear on the leader.

He knew that it was human nature not to want to charge an enemy who had repeating rifles aimed in your direction.

The Indians rode unshod ponies with hackamores. They had muzzle loader rifles, some spears, and knives. Three had bows. The bows would be the most dangerous at this range. By the time he or Tony could get off a second shot, they would have three arrows each heading in their direction.

The Indians began to talk loudly among themselves, spurred by a large brave. Their leader remained silent, his eyes fixed on Karl. The tension was almost explosive. Any move by Karl or Tony could start an attack. Karl's eyes did not waver from their leader.

"I am Karl August. We are bringing these horses to Fort Dakota and need you to let us pass. We do not want any trouble and will fight to the last man, if you make us." Karl kept his voice as commanding as he could.

Tony sat tall beside his brother. He had chosen the loud brave for his first shot. Hearing Karl's strong words had brought a strange calmness over him.

Karl tensed his legs, ready to attack. He would shoot the leader before he spurred his horse ahead.

"Auugus," the leader said. "You are Auugus?"

It took the brothers a moment to realize what the Indian had said, or that he even spoke in English.

"Yes, we are both August. As I said, I am Karl August. This is my brother Tony August."

The Indians around them began to shout something at their leader. It was evident they wanted to attack. Their leader held his hand up, and with a sharp command that the brothers did not understand, he silenced the other braves.

Slowly, the leader moved his horse toward Karl and Tony. The distance was less than a horse length.

"I am Haat-Nina-Auugus of the Ho-Chunk tribe. My mother Huhawira-Nina. My father from your people, a man named Auugus. He called my mother Nina. I not meet him, but my mother said he great man."

Karl and Tony looked at each other, wondering what the Indian was talking about. The leader spoke English, but what he said made little sense. All the brothers knew for sure was that the leaders defensive posture had disappeared.

"Our father, Oli August was also a great man," Karl said trying to keep a conversation going. He continued to keep an eye on the other braves that hadn't lessened their defensive postures.

Haat-Nina-Auugus lifted an emblem tied to a leather string around his neck. "My father give this to my mother. She give to me. It protect me from evil."

Tony cocked his head and then turned to Karl. "That has the same shape of the engraving on father's ledger."

Karl nodded, and slowly reached back and withdrew the ledger from his saddle bag. Showing it to Haat-Nina-Auugus, Karl pointed to the depression in the center of the cover. He could see the holes on the top and bottom that had once held rivets. Looking at the Indians emblem, he could see the remainder of a rivet in the bottom hole. The top rivet had been removed to insert the string.

Could it be they had the same father? He saw Tony staring wide-eyed at the emblem. No doubt his brother had come to the same conclusion.

Karl wished that he could step back and figure this thing out. Here he was, surrounded by Indians, with what appeared to be his brother sitting in front of him. He did recall his father talking about helping an Indian woman while he wandered the wilderness.

In a matter-of-fact tone, the Indian leader spoke. "Call me Haat. My mother told me of a vision. Someday, I meet other sons of Auugus. She had me learn your tongue from monks, so we could speak when we met. She and my father did not share a tongue."

Haat noticed Karl and Tony's discomfort being surrounded by the other Ho-Chunks. "I will send others away. We have much to talk."

With a motion of his hand, the other braves moved back, grumbling amongst themselves.

Tony blurted out, "Karl . . . ah, Haat, I should go back and let Josh know what is going on. I will be right back."

Turning his horse, Tony slowly rode back to the herd. He did not want to startle Josh and have him send the horses running. He quickly explained to Josh that it appeared everything was alright and that he should hold the horses here. He then trotted his horse back to Haat and Karl.

Sitting around a small fire with Tony and Haat, Karl made a pot of coffee. He also put out some biscuits from breakfast. Haat stared at them as they began to pour the coffee. They only had two cups, so Karl offered his to Haat.

"No," he replied. "Coffee smells good. I don't like taste."

Karl thought, *Good, then we have enough cups.* "How did your mother meet our father?" Tony asked.

Haat stared into the distance. "My mother was taken from our village by people from the west. She escaped. Traveled for many days with them after her. She finally get away. By then, she was without food for many days. She make fire to cook what she can catch. She was too weak to hunt. A wild cat picked up her smell. It try to make a meal of her. Just as cat leaped at her, Auugus with hair of gold come with only knife and stick, he chase cat off. This man then cared and fed my mother until she was strong."

"They traveled toward the rising sun, to find my mother's people. Sharing their blankets at night for warmth and comfort. One morning my mother look for the food. She meet those from her village. She fear for my father and lead them away. Away from the one with golden hair."

"Later, one of my uncles go back to see if someone followed. It is said he was killed by my father. My father showed great respect for uncle after fight. My mother got the others to return to village. She told them the man with golden hair had strong medicine with gods and a knife like lightning from sky."

Karl and Tony sat, absorbing what Haat had told them. The story their father had also told them had left out the warmth and comfort part. They no longer had any doubt. The Ho-Chunk Indian whom they were looking at was their brother.

"We are bringing these horses to Fort Dakota to earn money. The money will be used to bring cattle from Texas to Kansas City," Karl began to explain. "We need to get money to help our mother. Without it, she will lose her land. The land of our father. We will sell the cattle and then make our father's land secure."

He didn't know if Haat understood exactly what he was saying, but he needed him to understand that they had no horses to spare.

"You say you going to Fort Dakota?" Haat asked, nodding. "We will help. We protect you from Sioux and others who would take horses."

With that, Haat returned to the other Ho-Chunk braves and explained the plan. Then, as a group, they rounded up the horses and got them moving back toward Fort Dakota. Josh looked mighty uncomfortable being surrounded by Ho-Chunk Indians.

Tony rode over to him and said, "Don't worry, Josh. My brother will take care of us." And he proudly pointed to Haat.

The next week and a half went by smoothly, except for one incident. Shortly after starting one hazy morning, a small band of Sioux tried to scatter and raid the horses.

Tony and Josh were the closest to the raiders and opened fire with their rifles. Karl, who was riding drag, spurred his horse forward and emptied his Army Colt as he rode up. The sudden barrage of gunfire was too much for the Sioux, and they disappeared over a rise.

Haat and the other Ho-Chunks did an excellent job of keeping the frightened horses bunched and prevented a stampede.

The Ho-Chunks took care of driving the horses by day and guarding them at night. Their camp was set just to the side of the boys. Karl and Tony were able to spend a lot of time hunting and supplied everyone with meat.

Josh stayed with the horses or close to camp, watching over his father's interest. He was not able to fully trust the Indians and expected them to spirit the horses away at any moment.

Karl, Tony, and Haat spent many hours learning about each other. They crossed the Sioux River on the twelfth day after meeting. The fort was about a day's ride north of them. With the help of the Indians, they had not lost a single horse. The horses were in great shape, having good feed the entire trip.

Haat met with Karl and Tony. "The braves want to continue on the hunt for buffalo. It be easy driving horses from here."

Karl stood with his hat in his hand. "Haat, we do not have anything to give you and your people for the help given to us. I would offer you some horses, but they are not mine to give."

Haat smiled at his brother. "You owe nothing. Meeting you brothers gives strong medicine. It make buffalo hunt success. My mother say our father came to her from sun. He had hair of gold on face and head. His eyes were from sky. He has shared this with you, Karl. As long as you are well, the Ho-Chunk will have food and health."

Tony cleared his throat. "Haat, be careful how you talk to Karl. His head will swell and his hat won't fit."

They stood with Josh watching the Ho-Chunks ride away from the river, heading west. They waved to the departing braves, and Haat sat tall on his horse and held his arm straight in the air, pointing at the sun.

CHAPTER 4

Fort Dakota was located on the western bank of the Sioux River, not far from the falls. There was a combination of log and stone buildings. They were directed to bring the horses into a pasture behind the livery stable.

Once done, they tied their horses at a rail near the corral and loosened the cinches. A young second lieutenant named Sparks signed and gave them the receipt for the horses.

"You brought all 50 through. We are damn glad of that. The Sioux have been giving us fits and we have been short of horse flesh." He pointed at a stone building. "The purser's office is near the commissary. Bring this to him and he will cut you a draft that you can draw on a bank when you get home."

Karl raised his hand to get the lieutenant's attention. "Hold on, Lieutenant Sparks, we need cash. We are going from here to Texas. Only part of the money is mine to take. The rest goes back to Elkader."

Shrugging his shoulders, the young lieutenant began to walk away. "Can't help you boys. I only sign the receiver." Karl grabbed at the lieutenant's arm, but he shook it off.

Turning to Josh, Karl asked, "Your father said we would be paid when we delivered the horses. Did he give you money to do that?"

By the look on Josh's face, Karl knew that he was as surprised as they were. With the receiver safely in Karl's money belt, the three walked across the compound toward the commissary.

"Hey August! Karl August! What the hell you doing in this area? You plan to join back up?" Walking toward them was a red-headed officer. He had rosy round cheeks and was carrying a few extra pounds under the tight-fitting uniform.

Tony noticed his brother instinctively straighten a bit. "Major Thomas, it is good to see you."

The major put his arm around Karl's shoulder. "We miss you out here, captain. The Sioux have been giving us an awful time."

Tony looked at his brother. He had never told him that he was an officer. Tony suddenly had even more respect for his older brother.

"We got us a problem, major. We just delivered horses and we can only get a draft against an eastern bank. We need cash to head for Texas," Karl said.

"Damn, you do have a problem," the major said. "Up until a couple months ago I could have helped you without any trouble. We had a change of command, and now I am just waiting around for orders."

The major looked at Tony and Josh like he was deciding if they were boys or men. Decision made, he slapped Karl on the shoulder. "I know this place that has rye that won't make you go blind. Come with me and let me buy you men a drink."

They trooped into a low log building. A wide plank was supported between two flour barrels. The shelf behind the bar had a row of bottles with a light brown liquid. The room smelled of cigar smoke, sweat, and spilt rye.

"Set my friends up with some glasses and a bottle, Lou," the major said.

The lanky bartender had a long, turkey-like neck and ears that could be used for sails. "Sure thing, major. The wife just finished cooking a nice bear roast. I can put out a feed if you want."

Looking at Karl, the major said, "You men hungry?"

He got a round of agreement and they chose a table. Soon they had heaping plates of roast bear meat, beans, and large slices of fresh bread.

Tony looked at the major. "Damn, this is good grub. We've been eating Josh's cooking for three weeks. Not saying that he doesn't do well over a cook fire, but this guy's wife has the knack."

Licking his lips, Josh said, "Tony, I have to agree with you. Mighty tasty meal."

The major poured a round of drinks. Raising his glass, he toasted them. "Here's to good food, good whiskey, and friends."

Drinking down the shot, the major continued. "This brother of yours is the reason I am here or anywhere today. He was my right-hand man when we went out hunting for cattle to feed the men. We came up against three Confederate soldiers that took exception to our taking their stock."

"There we were" he said, "caught flat-footed, and them with the drop on us. I was bracing for a belly full of lead when Karl here jumped his horse into the nearest soldier. I heard three shots and was relieved to see the three Confederates flat on their backs, headed for the next world. Your brother just slipped his Army Colt in his holster and continued on pushing those cows."

Laughing and talking, the major kept them entertained with stories about him and Karl in the war. Tony noticed that his brother wasn't completely comfortable with the stories. Karl had always believed that you do what is expected and necessary. Once done, there was no need to remind folks that you had done it.

The bartender's wife brought a blackened pot of strong, hot coffee to wash the meal down. She was a portly gal with a stained apron, and salt and pepper hair tied back with a rag. When she smiled, she had several teeth missing. The boys did not mind, though, because that woman could cook.

After a bit too much to drink, the three left the tavern. It was dark. Karl wondered where the afternoon had gone. The major followed them out after having a few words with Lou. Karl looked at the corral rail. Their horses were missing!

The major called after them. "Don't worry about your horses. I had some boys put them up in the stable. They had a good rubdown and a generous helping of oats. You head for the barracks and grab a billet for the night. You will find your gear there. I'll see you guys in the morning."

Karl walked toward the barracks, wondering how he could have forgotten to go back and take care of the horses. A man depends on his mount and it should be taken care of first. Not getting the cash and running into the major had thrown him off. He made a mental note not to let it happen again. With full stomachs and many days in the saddle, all three were ready to crawl into bed.

Karl woke up just before sunrise. After using the latrine, he walked over to the pump and washed up. He leaned against the barrack's wall and took out a cigar the major had given him. Striking a match, he lit the cigar and settled down for a quiet smoke, watching the sun come up.

"Not much of a breakfast."

Surprised, Karl looked over at the prettiest girl he could remember seeing. She had red, shoulder-length hair and green eyes. There was a sprinkle of freckles across her cheeks. She had a blanket wrapped over her shoulders to keep the morning chill off. Even with the blanket, Karl could tell that she had a shapely figure.

"I'm sorry," she apologized. "I didn't mean to startle you. My name is Karen Thomas. I am the major's niece. His brother, my father, was killed during the Civil War and he has taken care of me since."

Karl remembered when the major's brother was killed. There had been a brief skirmish with some Confederates. They'd pushed the line back to join up with his brother's company. When the fighting was over the major had been notified that his brother had been wounded.

He'd asked Karl to come with him to the surgeon's tent. Karl had had to steel his stomach as he walked by stacks of arms and legs tossed into a hole behind the tent. The ground was sticky with blood, and the smell of death and decay was everywhere.

The major was sent to a farmhouse just up the hill from the tent. They'd found his brother lying on a large, wood frame bed with an overstuffed mattress. He'd been cleaned up, but dying. There was no fix for stomach wounds, just a painful and slow death.

His brother had been given opiates and had not been aware of their presence.

"Go back to the men, captain, and make sure they are fed and taken care of. I want to stay here for a while," the major had said.

Karl had nodded. "Don't worry about the men, sir. I will take care of things." Karl remembered being glad to leave the dead and dying and going back to camp.

Snapping back to the present, Karl took a deep drag on the cigar. "I'm Karl, and you are right, Miss Thomas. This is not the best breakfast. Had a bit to drink last night and I am trying to clear the cobwebs. Oh, and you are welcome to startle me anytime."

Karen turned to watch the sun come up. "This is my favorite time of the day. Things are so quiet and uncomplicated. My uncle told me about last night. He said you served with him. Did you know my father?"

Feeling rather uncomfortable, Karl nodded. "Yes, I met your father once briefly."

"The major said he died quickly and bravely," she said.

Agreeing, Karl said, "I am sure he died without pain."

Shaking her red curls, Karen turned. "Follow me, Captain August. I know where we can find some fresh coffee."

Karl followed her, a bit surprised that she used his last name. He wondered what else the major had told her. They entered a small room in the commissary, set up for guests of the fort. Before going in, Karl placed his cigar on a rock near the door. Two men in clean white uniforms moved quickly to set up a table and pour them coffee.

The taller of the two leaned forward before going. "Breakfast will be served in one hour. Would you like to place your orders now?"

Karl had not had this type of service since he'd gotten out of the army. The officers had been treated quite well when out in the field.

"Yes, thank you," Karen said. "We will have eggs and ham. Could we please get some sweet bread right away?"

"Certainly, Miss Thomas," the man in white said as he left the room.

"I hope it was okay to order breakfast for you, captain," Karen said, covering her mouth, surprised at her boldness.

"It is not a problem. I couldn't choose better company to eat with, but you must stop calling me captain. I am out of the Army, and it is just Karl."

Before he had a chance to take another sip of the coffee, the man in white was back with assorted sweet breads. The coffee was not as strong as Karl liked, but the sweet breads definitely made up for it.

Karl enjoyed talking with Karen. She told him about her life traveling with the army. Her mother had died of cholera when she'd been very young. She had spent much of her time in boarding schools for ladies. What she'd liked best was when she was out of school and with her father. She was able to ride with western-style saddles. She enjoyed mingling with the ladies at the forts. Everything was so much less formal than the schools.

Karl told her about Elkader, about his home on the Turkey River, also about his family. He even found himself telling her about the plan to drive cattle up from Texas.

"It sounds exciting. I wish I could do something like that," Karen said, tilting her head back just a bit.

You are in way over your head with this one, Karl thought. With breakfast done, he excused himself. "I have to meet the other two men I am traveling with. We have some business to do before we leave the fort."

Touching her hand momentarily, Karl turned and went outside, quickly picking up the cigar as he passed the rock. He was leaning against the corral when Tony and Josh found him.

"We didn't see you at breakfast, Karl. They had all the porridge you could eat. Weren't you hungry? " Tony asked.

"I had breakfast with an angel," Karl said, smiling from ear to ear.

With confused expressions on their faces, Tony and Josh followed Karl to the purser's office. A corporal in a neatly pressed uniform sat behind the desk. He looked the receiver over.

"Major Thomas said you needed cash. Well, you are in luck. We happen to have enough to cover the receiver. Just sign here."

Relief flooded over Karl. "Josh, you have to sign for the money," Karl said.

Awkwardly, Josh walked up to the table and signed the receipt of cash document.

Josh looked at the corporal. "I need to send two thousand of this to my father in Elkader, Iowa."

The corporal glared at the three. "More damn paperwork. You should have told me that to begin with. Here, I'll need you to fill out a deposit of cash. Then I need you to fill out a transfer of cash so I can send a draft to your father. He will then be able to draw it on a bank in Elkader."

Karl and Tony watch the corporal and Josh work out the necessary paperwork to transfer the money. Karl smiled at Tony and patted the $500 in the money belt around his waist. This and the money he had hidden in his saddle bags should get them through.

The three men went to the commissary to purchase items that they would need for the trip south. They used some of the $500 to purchase 400 rounds of rimfire cartridges for the Henry rifles. Josh had picked up 100 rounds for his Sharps. The old gent at the commissary had laughed and asked them if they were expecting a war. Karl knew how fast ammunition could be used up in a firefight.

Josh was still looking over some things when the brothers settled up. "I will be right along," he promised.

Waving to Josh, Karl and Tony headed for the stable to saddle the horses. "We will have to sleep with one eye open, carrying so much money." Tony commented.

"Lots of folks traveling along the river, and most carry only enough to eat," Karl replied. "We need to stay alert, but I wouldn't worry too much."

Arriving at the stable, Karl was surprised to see Karen. She was standing by the corral watching a mare with a new colt. "Isn't it beautiful?" she called to him.

Tony continued into the stable to ready the horses. Walking over to Karen, Karl leaned against the rail. "It is, and there seems to be a lot of that around here."

Realizing how dumb his statement must sound, Karl blushed with embarrassment. The young red-head took it as a compliment and whispered, "Thank you."

"We have to get going," he said. "It will take three days riding to get to Sioux City."

"Could I ask you one favor?" she said with a coy smile.

"Uh, sure," he replied. "If I can do it, I will."

"Join me for a picnic down by the river before you leave," Karen said. "All I ask is an hour of your time."

Tony came out of the stable leading his horse. "Do you want me to saddle the black?"

"Yes. Yes, if you would, Tony," he replied. "No hurry, though. I have something important to do and will be back in about an hour."

His younger brother had a smirk on his face as he watched Karl and Karen leave the stable. They stopped briefly at her quarters and she came out with a basket, packed and ready. "What would you have done if I had said I had to go?" he asked.

"The thought never crossed my mind," she replied.

Karl hardly touched the fried chicken she had packed for them as they sat on the river bank. While he knew of the urgency to get started, it would be okay if they spent the rest of the afternoon together. Karen laughed and talked about her dreams. While Karl usually found it difficult to engage with the ladies, he found her very easy to talk with.

True to her word, shortly after the hour was over, she said, "It is time to go back. We didn't do the meal justice. I will send it with you and Tony."

They found Josh and Tony waiting in front of the commissary. They were thrilled with the food. Karen gave Karl a quick hug and hurried away, promising to wait for his return. Struggling to regain his composure, he fussed with the horse, double checking his gear.

Major Thomas met them as they got ready to leave the fort. "I know you plan to drive the cattle to Kansas, but if you decide to keep moving them up here, you will get a third more for them. The army always needs meat, and we are stuck up here, a bit off the normal routes for supplies."

Karl thanked him for the thought. "If things work out, we just might drive them here. I hope time will allow it."

Taking Karl aside, the major told him, his normally booming voice much lower. "I will leave word for you here if the orders come through before we see you again and let you know where we have gone. Any letters you send here will be forwarded to my new command."

"I hope you get orders soon, so you can get settled into that new command," Karl said, shaking the major's hand.

The major laughed and slapped his knee. "You know the army. Once I get the orders, they will want me to hurry along. In the meantime, they want me to wait. Who knows, if you get back up here before I get orders, there is someone who would be waiting to see you again."

Karl blushed and climbed into the saddle. "Until next time, major."

The major stood and watched the three men ride out of sight. "Yes sir, he would make a fine husband for that niece of mine," he reflected.

The young Karen Thomas, watching them from a window as they rode away, could not agree more.

CHAPTER 5

The Big Sioux River ran from the fort to Sioux City. Major Thomas had told them that a steamboat ran from there to St. Louis. It would take three days to reach the boat landing. The rutted road following the river skirted most of the swampy areas, with only a few smaller ones filled in with logs.

It was late May, and Karl knew that they had to get cattle rounded up in Texas and start the drive before it got too dry. He figured to hunt the cattle up in the Waco area. Karl was familiar with the area from his time in the war. Starting from there, the drive would take them just over two months to Kansas City. He knew that it would take another month to continue up to Fort Dakota if they decided to go for higher prices.

Spring flowers covered the hills around them, giving splashes of blue and yellow. The mornings would be filled with the sounds of songbirds and the nights with frogs and crickets.

Their time at the fort had been short, and meeting Karen had distracted Karl from doing some of the things that needed done. For one thing, his Colt and Henry rifle needed cleaning. The army had taught him that the condition of a weapon could be the difference between life and death. A misfire against an advancing enemy gave them the advantage.

The three men, rode enjoying the late spring weather. Tony and Josh kept up a constant chatter as they talked excitedly about riding the steamboat to St. Louis. Karl was with his own thoughts, realizing the importance of the trip they were making.

They traveled for four hours the first day, stopping in a grove of cedar, which shielded them from the road. The sun was low in the sky as they enjoy the fried chicken and sweet bread sent by Karen. They build a small fire to brew coffee.

They were up at first light and back on the road. Josh spotted a large brown mass slowly moving across the grass-covered plain. "Look at all the buffalo!" he exclaimed. "The Ho-Chunks could finish their hunt in a hurry with that herd."

Given the time, they all would have liked to try taking down one of the large wooly beasts, but they needed to keep riding. They stopped on a rocky rise to give the horses a breather and eat a midday meal of jerky and water. To the east the sun glimmered off the river, and to the west the new grass was an ocean of green.

They chose a wooded area next to the river to camp the second night. Josh offered to collect wood and start the fire, while the brothers pulled the gear off the horses. Once the fire was going, the coffee water was put on and a pot of beans to boil.

"I think we should do some fishing," Josh suggested. "If we're lucky, we might catch enough for supper and have some left for breakfast."

Tony laughed, "Damn, Josh. You must have a fish-catching secret you never told me about."

The two of them headed for a willow tree to make some rods, while Karl dug under rocks and rotting logs for worms. Using a piece of dry stick for their bobbers, the two friends sat on the river bank, waiting for a hungry fish to strike.

Karl looked around their camp. It was off the road far enough to prevent someone passing by from seeing them. The trees and brush gave them plenty of cover. At the same time, it would provide the same for anyone trying to get close to the camp.

Josh came back from the river holding several fat catfish, using a stick for a stringer. "Get me the frying pan out of our packs, Karl. We will eat well tonight."

The sweet meat of the fish went well with the beans. When the meal was done, they all went to the river to wash their dishes. The coffee pot was kept next to the coals for later. Coming back to the camp, Karl dug out what he needed to cleaned his Henry and Colt while Tony and Josh stayed down by the river.

Sitting around the fire after dark, they heard the lonely howl of wolves, calling to each other as they hunted the weak or young buffalo. They let the fire burn down to avoid drawing attention to the camp.

Karl made it a point not to look into the campfire. Their father had warned them of this when he took them on trips to the woods. He'd always said that the few seconds it takes your eyes to adjust to darkness could be fatal. He'd also taught them to keep their fires small.

During the evening, the air had cooled quickly. The clear, star-studded sky assured the men that they wouldn't have to worry about rain. They huddled around the glowing coals with their coats on, drinking the last of the coffee.

After checking on the horses, they spread their blankets under a willow tree. Karl put the money belt and his Colt under his saddle. His rifle was just under the edge of the blanket, to keep the night dew off. He was pleased to see that Tony and Josh did the same.

The first light of morning was showing across the river when Karl awoke. He laid for a moment listening to the even breathing of Tony and Josh. He noticed that heavy clouds had moved in during the night. He wanted to get an early start, figuring that they could eat the leftover fish and coffee for breakfast.

Grabbing the Colt, he stuck it into the waist band and, stocking footed, he moved a short distance away from the camp to relieve himself. Finishing up, he noticed that the woods were quiet. He felt a tingling in his back. It was the same feeling that he'd often gotten while in the army. Something wasn't right.

Adjusting the Colt, he headed back to the camp to wake Tony and Josh. He had a feeling that they were being watched. It could be marauding Indians looking to steal horses or guns. Hurrying back to the camp, he found the two men sitting up in their blankets, covered by the guns of two men!

"You best drop the gun in your belt or we'll shoot the boys here," a scruffy-looking stranger warned.

The two men were dressed in ill-fitting army pants and shirts, and had tattered hats pulled down low over their brows. Both had several days growth of whiskers, but the revolvers they held in their hands were clean and cocked.

Karl hesitated a moment, and the man covering Josh struck the boy across the top of the head, knocking him to the ground. "Drop it, or I shoot the kid!"

Knowing that if he tried anything but laying down his Colt, one or both of the boys would be killed. Placing the Colt onto the ground, Karl stepped away from it. "Don't harm the boys. I did what you asked."

"Sid, get their guns," the man with his gun on Tony instructed his partner.

Karl stood helpless while Sid went through the camp and collected up the guns. A broad smile came across his face when he lifted Karl's saddle and saw the money belt.

"Look what I found," he bragged to his partner, holding it up.

The man kept Karl's Henry repeater, but threw the other rifles and revolvers into the river. His partner kept the drop on the men. Before finishing their search, they tied Karl's and Tony's hands with pigging strings. Josh remained unconscious on the ground next to his blankets.

While the brothers sat and watched, the men dug through the packs, keeping a few items that they liked. Then Sid went and got the horses off the picket line. Anger coursing through him, Karl sat, holding his tongue. Saying anything at this time could get them killed.

Sid's partner sneered at the bound men. "Thank you for your hospitality."

They left, leading the three horses. There were shouts as they sent the horses running down the road. They then heard the thieves galloping away with the money belt. Before the sounds of the departing horses faded, Karl had the Good Knife from the nape of Tony's neck and they freed themselves.

Karl headed for the river to find the guns, while Tony checked on Josh. He had found the Navy Colt and the Sharps rifle when Tony came down to the river. "Josh has a hell of a knot on his head. I got him awake, but looks like he'll need some time. Give me those guns and I'll clean them while you find a horse."

Returning back to camp, Karl pulled on some dry socks and his boots. He saw that Tony had gotten Josh back under his blankets. "Look for the other guns after you clean these," he told his brother.

Karl left the camp at a run. He got to the road and saw the bay, a quarter-mile down, looking back in his direction. Luck was with him. As he got closer, he saw that all three horses had stopped and were grazing on a patch of grass. Their lead ropes trailed alongside them.

He whistled, and the gelding lifted its head and trotted toward him. Walking slowly, Karl held out his hat and the black was easily caught, expecting a treat. Grabbing the horse's mane, he jumped onto the animal's back and began herding the other horses toward their camp.

Tony had the Navy Colt and Sharps ready to go. He was waist-deep in the river, feeling with his feet for the other guns. Karl saddled the black and stuck the Sharps into his scabbard. After a quick check to make sure that the other money was still there, he put the saddle bags and bed roll on the horse. His brother came up with the rest of the guns.

Not wanting to waste any more time cleaning his revolver, he said, "I'm going to take your Colt, Tony. I got some additional loads out of our packs. I also got Josh's Sharps."

At the sound of his name, the young man in the blankets moaned. Tony hurried to him. "Glad to see you're awake. You had us worried."

"My head feels like it was split open," Josh groaned.

Karl stood next to the two young men. "I'm going after our money. Once Josh is able to ride, I want you two to continue to Sioux City. The men thought the belt had all our money. I'll keep what's in my saddle bags. You can use Josh's money to get to St. Louis and find Albert and James. You just keep going as we planned, and if I don't catch up to you before, I will meet you in Waco."

"If I am delayed, start the roundup and drive the cattle to Kansas City. I figure I'll be back long before that," he said, knowing that it just might be necessary if things went bad for him. Both brothers knew that the home in Elkader would be lost without the cattle drive.

Swinging onto the black, Karl rode out of camp, unable to look at the worry on his brother's face. Tony was young, but he was man size and Karl knew that he could bring the cattle to market with the help of Albert and Josh. He was not so sure of James Wolfe.

Without the horse money, they would have to depend on the money James carried. He knew the drive could be delayed in St. Louis if James held back. It would be his right according to the contract. Karl knew if he showed up in St. Louis without the money and found everyone waiting, then as a last ditch effort he could telegraph their mother to send what she could. He knew weeks would be lost in the process. Deciding it would do no good to keep these thoughts in his mind, Karl focused on following the thieves.

He stopped at the road where the men had tied their horses. The tracks went directly west, across the prairie, as they'd ridden away. There was little that they would find in that direction, except the Missouri River and a lot of rolling prairie. To get any pleasure out of the money that they had stolen, they would have to go north to the fort, or south to Sioux City.

The men had a three-hour start. Karl took a drink from his canteen and dug out a piece of jerky. It would have to do for his breakfast. He moved out on the black with grim determination on his face. He would track these men down, or die trying.

The tracks here were easy to follow on the spring prairie grass. The men had kept on a straight route, heading west. After a mile at a gallop, the men had slowed their horses to a walk. He kept the black at a trot, wondering about the men he was following.

Had they shot the three of them, they would not have had to worry about being followed. Karl had seen a lot of killing in the war and knew that not every man could shoot another. Hitting Josh over the head might have been part of their plan to delay pursuit. Any way one looked at it, it had reduced the number of riders chasing them.

Around mid-afternoon, Karl came to a rock formation jutting up from the prairie grass. The men had stopped just short of it. Swinging down from the black, he took a closer look at something lying in the grass. It was the money belt!

Karl looked in the empty belt, wondering why it had been discarded. Shortly, along the trail he found out. The men had split the money and one had ridden north while the other had gone south. He sat on the black, looking at the two trails, and muttered, "What the hell do I do now?"

While he had asked himself the question, he knew what had to be done. The man riding south was heading for Sioux City. The other was bringing the money further away from their destination. Turning the black north, he brought it to a trot.

The tracks he was following were less than two-hours old. He had made up almost half the lead. The man he followed was still traveling at a walk. Suddenly, he knew why. The man had ridden into a wide swath of prairie chewed up by the hooves of grazing buffalo. It was impossible to pick the horses tracks from the buffalo.

The torn-up ground extended over a mile ahead of Karl. He pondered his options. The thieves tended to ride in a straight line. If the man continued to ride in the direction he was now heading he would end up in the badlands. If he had been aware of the buffalo moving through this area, he would have waited until reaching it and then turned.

Deciding that the man was heading for the fort, Karl headed the black in a northeasterly direction and forgot about looking for tracks. After leaving the chewed-up grass, he began to travel rougher terrain.

It was late afternoon and the black was beginning to tire. For the last hour he had kept it at a walk. He was a little over four hours from the fort. To the east he could catch glimpses of the river.

Without warning, something struck him under his arm, followed by the report of a rifle. The impact knocked him off the horse. Karl struggled for breath, hugging the ground, expecting another bullet at any second. His hat lay several feet away.

He looked for any cover around him. There was none close. Another bullet struck some ledge just over his head, showering him with bits of rock. He could feel blood running down his side, and it hurt to breath. Daring not to look, he feared that the first bullet had penetrated a lung.

Just as another bullet struck the ledge and whined away, Karl leaped up, running, fear and adrenaline carrying him as he made for an outcrop that would give him some cover. As he ran, Karl was aware of shots being fired.

The man was using a repeater rifle, probably his own Henry. Karl hit the ground behind the outcrop, the pain of the wound almost paralyzing him. He reached for the Navy Colt. His first attempt was stopped by the loop. Removing it, he drew the gun.

He looked around for his horse. The animal had run east and he could see it in a shallow valley. If he tried to run for the horse, he would be an open target for a hundred yards. Another bullet ricocheted off the rock in front of him causing him to duck.

He doubted that he could even run the distance, having been shot. Listening for any movement of someone coming his way, Karl checked the wound under his right arm. The bullet had torn a long gash about six inches below his armpit. He was thankful. It might have cracked a rib, but he wasn't carrying a bullet. He withdrew his bloody fingers, wiping them on the rocks.

Removing his bandanna, he folded it and held it in place with his arm. Karl shot with his right hand, but had practiced shooting with both hands during the war for just this type of instance.

The shooting had stopped. Either the man was working his way closer, or had figured Karl had been hit hard enough and had abandoned the fight. He worked his way to the edge of the outcrop and tried to see where the man might be shooting from. There were a number of places that the man could use for cover.

Motion caught his eye. The man had gone over a small rise leading his horse. The bushwhacker had abandoned the fight. Putting the Colt into his waistband to keep it handy for his left hand, Karl got up, supporting himself with the outcrop.

After picking up his hat, a whistle brought the black back toward him. Karl was unable to stand straight due to the pain of the wound. Slowly, he walked to the horse, gripping the saddle horn with his left hand and swinging onto the horse.

His attention was on a rise to his east. It would give him a good view of the uneven terrain ahead of him. He was thankful that the black had a smooth gait. Every slight jar sent shooting pains through his side.

Gaining the rise, Karl got off the horse and pulled the Sharps .50 caliber. Using a waist-high ledge for support, he watched. Twice, he caught a brief look at the man he was following. He was thankful for the cloud cover, keeping down the glare.

He had removed his shirt and had tied it around his chest to hold the folded bandana against his side. A quarter-mile away there was a shelf that the rider would have to cross. The rifle in his hands had an effective range to the shelf and a maximum range of much more.

One of the duties that Karl had had in the army had been as a sniper. One of the rifles he had used was the Sharps. Flipping up the ladder sight, he waited. With his elbow resting on the ledge, he put the rifle against his right shoulder. He prayed that if a second shot was needed, he would be able to load and fire.

From Karl's vantage point it looked like the thief would offer a broad back shot when he gained the shelf. Then would have to ride across it to the right, giving the horse a broad side shot. All Karl knew was that the man was not going to ride off the rocky shelf.

As he waited, Karl's eyes began to get heavy, fearing that it was due to blood loss. He wished that he could wash his eyes, but the canteen was on the horse and he didn't dare leave to get it. He would only have a short time to take the shot. Karl knew that if the man made it over the shelf, the robber would win.

Sudden movement to the east of the shelf caught his eye. It was the rider going through another notch. Karl realized that he would get only one shot. He could only see the man's head and shoulders. Karl held his breath, waiting for more of the target to appear. As the thief's horse went over a low ridge, the man's full back was exposed.

Karl put the sights onto his target and squeezed the trigger. A full second later the man's arms went out from his sides and he fell from the horse, disappearing behind the ridge. Blinding pain wracked Karl's chest, causing him to go to his knees, dropping the rifle onto the ledge. For several minutes he waited for it to subside, and for the ability to take a full breath.

Even though the late afternoon was cool, Karl was covered with sweat. Struggling to get up, he used the rifle for support as he went to the horse. It would be dark soon, and other than knocking the man off the horse, he couldn't be certain that it was a kill.

Karl began to shiver. Before getting onto the horse, he put on his sheepskin vest. A fine mist began to fall. He thanked the Lord that the rain had held off until after he'd shot. Climbing onto the horse, he put on his rain slicker.

He had little to use as a landmark to keep him headed toward the notch, and found himself holding on to the saddle horn to keep from falling when the horse swayed. The rain was becoming harder, and there was the danger that the horse could slip on the wet rocks.

Finally, he saw the notch and the shelf to his left. He now realized that the shelf offered no access, forcing him toward the notch. Karl rode slowly, knowing that at any moment he would come upon the man, dead or alive. He felt too weak to get down and lead the black.

He saw the arm first. Slow and painfully, Karl dismounted. With the Colt in his hand, he approached the downed man. Sid lay with his mouth open and the rain falling into his sightless eyes. The Henry rifle lay on the rocks a few feet away. Karl heard the snort of the man's horse beyond the next rise.

Using the rock wall for support, Karl searched the dead man's pockets for the money. Sid had only a few dollars on him. It had to be on the horse. Karl pulled the Sharps from the scabbard. He opened the falling block and loaded the rifle. If Sid's horse ran, Karl would rather experience the pain from the kick of the Sharps than chase the horse.

It wasn't necessary. As Karl led the black over the ridge, Sid's horse walked toward him, welcoming the company. Karl found half of the money in the saddle bag. He put it back into the money belt and stuck it into the black's saddle bag.

A slanting rock wall offered some protection from the rain. Karl led the horses near the wall and tied them to a scrubby tree. He then got his bedroll and saddle bags off the black. For the next hour he slowly set up his camp for the night. He had a small fire to make coffee.

He just loosened the cinch on Sid's horse. He didn't have the energy to pull another saddle off a horse. He sat sipping coffee, thinking about the dead man not a hundred feet away. His first instinct was to leave the man to the wild animals.

Karl had seen hundreds of bodies left too long on the battlefield during the war. They would often be buried in shallow graves, their bones coming to the surface after a hard rain or from scavenging animals.

In the morning he would put the body onto the horse and, if he caught up with Tony and Josh, he would have them bury Sid. It would take too long to follow the tracks of the second thief, and there was a good chance that the rain would have washed them away.

Karl would look for the man in Sioux City. The man would assume that they were going there. It was very unlikely that he would be easily found.

Exhausted, he didn't do anything more with the wound. He just pulled his blanket over him and fell asleep. His dreams were about being back in the war. The rain continued to fall until shortly before daylight. When Karl awoke, he could hear water rushing in one of the normally dry river beds to the north.

He spent time washing and dressing the wound under his arm. The flesh around the gash was severely bruised. He soaked the bandana in a pot of hot water before using it to clean the area. Again, he used the shirt to keep a pad against the injury.

Karl drank coffee and ate hard bread for breakfast. The rest had done him well. While there was plenty of pain under his arm, he didn't feel as weak. After he got his gear onto the black, he led Sid's horse to the body.

It was all Karl could do to get the thief over the saddle. He rested a bit before tying Sid to the horse. It was well after daylight before he was on his way toward the road along the river. The Sharps rifle was in the scabbard and his Henry was cradled in his left arm. As he approached the road, he saw a wagon and several mounted soldiers coming from the south.

Fearing that he wouldn't get to the road before they passed, Karl fired two shots into the air, using the Henry. The riders scattered and dismounted while the men driving the wagon pulled it to a stop and got behind it.

Karl shouted a greeting to the soldiers and rode forward slowly, with his hands and the rifle in plain sight. The soldiers stood next to their horses at the ready, while their lieutenant and his sergeant waited at the front for Karl.

"My name is Karl August. The man over the horse behind me stole money from me and was shot during an exchange of fire," he explained.

The lieutenant walked forward, taking the Henry rifle. "Please dismount," he requested. Karl noticed that the sergeant remained back, holding a rifle that could be brought into action quickly.

Swinging his leg over the horse, Karl got down, gripping the saddle to steady himself. "This man's been wounded," the lieutenant called out. "Sergeant Kelly, bring the medical bag forward."

Then, to Karl, he said, "I do apologize, but I must also take your revolver before my man checks you over."

Slowly removing his Colt, Karl handed it to the officer. "I understand. I just got out of the army a year ago myself."

One of the soldiers was directed to take the horses, while another helped Karl to the crate that had been set next to the wagon. One of the soldiers with field training on wounds removed the shirt and pad.

"You're damn lucky, mister. A few inches over and you wouldn't need no doctoring," the soldier said.

While the wound was being cleaned and a proper dressing put on, the other soldiers took Sid's body from the horse. The lieutenant squatted next to the body, talking with one of his men. Then he and the soldier came back to the wagon.

"You say you shot the man," the lieutenant clarified.

"Yes, I did."

"Corporal Higgins here knew Sid Hoover. Sid was recently discharged out of the army," the officer informed Karl.

"I see he was back shot," the corporal sneered.

Giving him a steely look, Karl replied, "The coward and his friend stole my money and then Sid here bushwhacked me when I was tracking him down. He had no spine to come and finish me off, and was trying to sneak away when I put the bullet in him."

The lieutenant intervened, snapping, "Corporal, that will be all!"

Unconvinced, the angry soldier went back to Sid's body.

To Karl he apologized. "Higgins had no call to talk to you like that, Mr. August. You wouldn't be the Captain August that Major Thomas tells us stories about?"

"I was an officer in the major's command," Karl replied.

Looking back at the body, the lieutenant said, "Sid and his pal, Ray Scullin, were kicked out of the army in January. They had been hanging around the fort, causing their share of trouble while waiting for warm weather. Sid didn't know who he was tangling with when he went against you and that Sharps on the saddle."

The soldier who fixed the wound wrapped a tight bandage around Karl's chest to support the cracked rib. While it still hurt to breathe deep, normal movement didn't send shooting pains through him.

Taking a clean shirt out of his saddle bags, Karl put it on, along with the vest. The lieutenant handed him paper and a pencil to write a brief summary of what had caused Sid's death. Karl included Ray Scullin's part in the robbery.

"Can you take Sid off my hands?" he asked. "My brother and another man are headed to Sioux City, and I want to try and catch up to them."

"Captain, I'll do better than that," the lieutenant replied. "I'll have a detail bury the man and you can take his horse. Higgins asked if he could keep Sid's gear. I take it that the Sharps, and Henry, were both yours."

"The Henry is, and the Sharps belongs to the man with my brother. I know the army is always looking for horses," Karl told the lieutenant, "so I appreciate you letting me have it. My black is about wore out and I'll be able to ride faster switching horses."

The lieutenant invited him join them for a midday meal. Being anxious to start south, Karl declined. While he was switching his saddle to Sid's mustang, the officer sent two men to dig a grave for Sid.

Coming back, he told Karl, "Scullin had family with a small farm, a mile or so south of Sioux City. You said he rode south. That's where he would have been heading."

Thanking the lieutenant again, Karl climbed onto the mustang and headed out, leading his black. Sid's horse had a rougher gait, and he was thankful for the tightly wrapped ribs. A light rain began to fall, so Karl pulled on his slicker.

CHAPTER 6

It was dark, with a steady rainfall, when Karl got back to the wooded area where they had camped. Turning the horse in, he found it empty. Swinging off the horse, he led the black and mustang under the willow tree. It gave him some relief from the rain. Pulling the gear off, he picketed them in a grassy area near the river bank.

Searching under the trees, Karl found enough dry wood for his fire. Soon he had water heating for coffee. Chilled from the cold, damp weather, he put water into the frying pan and mixed cold flour to make a porridge.

The hot coffee and porridge warmed his insides. The rain working its way through the willow branches hissed when it hit the fire and spattered on his slicker. He sat against the trunk, drinking coffee and wondering when he would catch up to the others, or if he'd find Ray.

Slowly, as the fire died, Karl fell asleep, curling up in his rain slicker at the base of the tree. While he slept, using his arm for a pillow, the rain clouds moved to the east, allowing the stars to glow in the heavens.

Hours later he tried to move, his muscles protesting from sleeping in the damp slicker. It was first light when he opened his eyes. His breath caught as he looked directly at the buckskin-covered legs of an Indian. Without thinking, he spun away from the fire and drew his Army Colt.

"Brother! It is me!" Karl looked up into the face of Haat.

"For crying out loud, Haat, make some noise when you are coming to a man's camp. I might have shot you," he said, feeling sore and irritated.

Then he asked, "How did you find me?"

"I left other hunters to come and help with cattle. I found your black's trail a day ago. It easy to follow," Haat kidded. "I saw you with the soldiers and the body of a man. I was unsure of what had happened and didn't want to be seen by the army. Maybe they think I killed the man. I rode into the hills and waited for the soldiers to leave. They stay for long time and I thought you with them."

"When I hear them leaving, I watch and you were gone. I find the black's tracks going south. I see you are riding another horse and lead yours. I know you will stay on the road, so I not worry if rain washes the tracks. When darkness comes, I stop and rest. When light comes, I start again and heard your horses. I come here and find you sleeping."

"You should have come in when I was with the soldiers, Haat," Karl told him.

"My people, the Ho-Chunk, or as some know us, Winnebago, are being pushed west by the army," Haat explained. "They would ask me why I am in this area and may even make me stay with them to be taken west."

Karl was familiar with the conflict between the tribes and emigrants moving west. With the War Between the States over, there would be a flood of people looking for land or other riches. It could only mean more problems in the future.

The last thing Karl wanted to do was bring this kind of trouble with them. It would be difficult enough rounding up the cattle and driving them to the north.

"I thank you for the offer to come with us, my brother, but I don't think we will need more help," Karl said as kindly as he could.

"You will. With all the Comanche or Cherokee that will find you sleeping, you need me to warn you," Haat replied matter-of-factly.

Karl had watched Haat and how he handled the horses. He could read sign and fight like two men. The army had often used Indians as scouts during the war. Haat would be a good to have along.

Karl's only concern was the trip down to Texas. Indians were not readily accepted alongside white men. They would be traveling by steamboats.

As if reading Karl's mind, Haat continued. "I have friend who work on boats. They help with firing boilers and tending stock. It be good to see them on trip over the river." It was settled, then. Haat would be a very good addition to the venture.

Still chilled by the damp conditions, Karl put a fire together. Haat went and got his horse from near the road, then put his pinto with the other horses. Karl was huddled close to the fire, watching the coffee water slowly begin to steam, when Haat came up. He was carrying two rabbits.

"I used the bow and shot both of these before I started this morning," the proud Ho-Chunk said. "We eat them before we go."

With skilled hands, Haat cleaned the rabbits, and soon they were roasting over the fire skewered on willow sticks. Karl poured some hot water for tea into a cup for his Ho-Chunk brother before adding coffee grounds to the pot. While the meat roasted, they sat back and drank their coffee and tea.

"You were hurt," Haat stated. "I watch you favor your side."

"The dead man you saw with the soldiers shot me," Karl explained. "The soldiers fixed it for me."

"Tonight I will make something. It get better fast," the Ho-Chunk told him.

An hour later, the two men were riding south. They passed a cart being pulled by an ox. Karl asked the driver if he had passed any riders. The man said he had been on the road for two hours and hadn't seen anyone.

The sun was low in the western sky and Karl figured that they were about a half-day from Sioux City. He began to look for a spot to camp when he saw smoke from a fire. A sudden thought ran through his mind. What if it was Scullin?

Favoring a cautious approach, Haat stayed back while Karl rode slowly toward the camp. Relief flooded over him as he recognized Tony's and Josh's horses. He called back to Haat to come on in.

Hearing Karl, Tony and Josh came running from the river. "Am I glad to see you!" Tony shouted. Seeing the Ho-Chunk, he stopped, surprised. "You come with our brother."

The boys had a pot of beans with chunks of venison keeping warm on the edge of the fire. "You're just in time to join us for supper." Josh said. Soon, everyone was seated around the fire with plates of beans and biscuits. A pot of strong coffee sat by the fire, to enjoy after eating.

Between mouthfuls of food, Karl told them about tracking Sid and getting some of the money. Not wanting to make any of this Haat's problem, he planned to wait until later to tell Tony and Josh about Ray Scullin.

Tony explained that they had decided to camp here for a couple days before riding into Sioux City, hoping that Karl would catch up. The bump on the head had left Josh with a headache for a day, but he had no other ill effects.

They turned in right after the meal, wanting to get an early start. They awoke to a chilly north wind. The upside was that the sky had cleared, promising a warmer day. Anxious to get going, they ate a cold breakfast of leftover beans and cups of water. While Haat was taking care of the horses, Karl told Tony and Josh about Scullin. A half-hour after daylight, they were on the road.

Sioux City was a small town. The streets had been recently laid out and buildings were slowly being added. Many log structures were scattered about. Obviously, they were built before the city was planned.

They found that the next boat to St. Louis would leave in the morning. Haat waved to some men near the docks. "I see my friends. They will get me on boat," he assured Karl. "I will visit with them and see you in morning."

Bidding goodbye to his Ho-Chunk brother, Karl went to the ticket office to purchase needed passages and make arrangements for all the horses. He was told to have the animals at the boat two hours before departure.

Karl planned to sell the horses once in St. Louis. They would bring three times as much as a horse would cost in Texas. This was due to the demand that wagon trains were creating. Plus, their horses were not as well-trained for herding cattle as the Texas horses.

With tickets in hand, Karl caught up with Tony and Josh. They walked the horses over to a saloon and tied them to the rail out front. Karl looked up and down the street. There were deep ruts from recent rains. He could see puddles of water here and there. Some of the newer buildings had boardwalks in front.

The saloon was named Dekker's and had a small wooden porch in ill-repair. Because of the sunshine, the door was left open. Flies set up a constant buzzing in the front of the building. They walked in and crossed a plank floor that had seen better days. There was some sawdust scattered about. The place had a sour smell, from too many unwashed bodies and spilt drinks. The bar ran across the back wall. Karl noticed that someone had put some fine workmanship into building the bar.

The bartender was a short, nervous fellow who parted his hair in the middle. He had a stick with a flat piece of leather. He was busy slapping flies that landed on the bar.

"What'll it be, gents?" he asked as he slapped at a fly.

"Your sign behind the bar says 'cold beer'. We'll take three glasses of that."

The bartender drew three glasses and said, "That will be fifteen cents."

They moved over to a table to drink the beer. Karl could have debated with the man whether the beer was cold or not, but it did taste good.

"Are you the boys that rode in with the Injun?"

They turned and looked at a man sitting at the table near the window. He was medium height, had a baggy pair of wool pants and a greasy, sweat-stained shirt. His frayed hat hung by a string on his back. His gun was clean and in the holster on his right hip. Karl noticed that the loop was off the revolver. There was no doubt that the man had had too much to drink.

Karl repositioned himself at the table to give better access to his Colt before he replied. "We are, my friend. Can we buy you a beer?"

Karl hoped to disarm the situation with friendly conversation. He noticed that Tony had moved a bit and Josh was staring at the man with furled brows.

"Well boys, I don't drink with them that ride with Injuns," the drunk said. "Nope, I don't like 'em at all."

Karl noticed that the bartender had moved to the far end of the bar and was nervously polishing glasses.

"We really don't care what your feelings are about us riding with an Indian. We are just in here to have a beer and then we will be leaving." Karl spoke evenly, but inside he really wanted the guy to start something. If it wasn't for the possibility of Tony or Josh getting hurt, he would have braced the man.

Suddenly, the man staggered up, flipping his table over and poised his hand over his gun. Out of the corner of his eye, Karl saw Tony's arm move and he heard the Good Knife strike wood. Tony had pinned the man's arm to a post with his throw.

Jumping up, Tony relieved the man of his gun. Blood was running down the man's hand. Pulling the knife out, Tony shoved the drunk back into his chair.

"You don't hear so well, do you?" Tony said. "My brother was doing his best to save your life, and you just would not listen."

"My brother was in the war. He has been forced to kill better men than you. He does not think vermin like you are worth the cost of a bullet. Now, we are going to leave here and have some supper. We will leave your gun at the sheriff's office before we go in the morning. Personally I don't mind killing vermin, so, if you are so inclined, don't hesitate to come look me up."

In awe, Karl watched his brother pick up his beer and finish it. Wiping his mouth with the back of his hand, Tony nodded to Karl and Josh. "Let's go eat."

The drunk man sat staring at them from his chair, his face pale and his mouth hanging open.

They brought their horses to the livery to get them some grain and to ask about Scullin. The hostler was familiar with the name and the farm.

"Scullin's uncle is good folk," he told them. "But, Ray, he ain't worth the powder it would take to blow him away."

"Have you seen him around town?" Karl asked.

"Nah, haven't seen Ray," the man told them. "Course, he may be staying shy of town. He got in a little shooting trouble some time back and the sheriff might make things difficult for him."

They promised to return for the horses after they had some supper. The men walked up the street. The conversation came back to the man in the saloon.

"I sure am going to watch what I say to you from now on, Tony. I don't want that pig sticker in my arm," Josh said, pretending to be intimidated.

They all laughed and headed into Dixie's Café for some supper. They ordered steaks and potatoes and were soon busy carving them up, enjoying every bite.

Karl watched his brother during supper. He had seen Tony fight before, but that had been schoolyard-type fighting. Everyone knew that the worst that would happen was bumps and bruises.

Today, it had been life and death on the line. It bothered him that Tony has been put in danger, yet his quick moves had saved lives.

"Thank you for today, Tony," Karl said, pushing his plate away. He then said, "I believe you prevented the situation from getting out of hand."

Tony looked at his older brother. "I appreciate your words. I did it because I was scared. I knew you would have to kill him, and I was looking for a way out."

Karl looked at his brother and nodded. "Your actions were just right."

His thoughts went back to Sid and the war. Karl knew all too well what it felt like to look into the face of someone you had just killed.

After the meal they went and got the horses from the livery. They decided to camp outside of town under some cottonwoods. There was some grass nearby where they could picket the horses. Taking Tony aside, he told him, "I want you and Josh to wait here while I go and see if Scullin is at his uncles."

"Josh can stay here, but I am going with you, Karl," Tony said.

"We can't risk both of us being unable to go south," Kart said.

"When Josh was hurt, I could understand having to stay back, but it don't make any sense you going alone to face this Scullin," Tony said defiantly. "I was there to help you today and will do so tonight."

Overhearing the conversation, Josh piped up, "I am going also. You don't need anyone to watch an empty camp."

Overruled by the younger men with him, Karl gave in. There was still enough daylight left to get to the farm. The three of them headed out, riding abreast across the prairie grass.

They came to the small farm from behind the barn. Karl held his hand up for them to stop. Someone was going into the house with an armload of wood. It was Ray Scullin!

"Josh, I want you to go around to the back of the house, in case there is another door. If Scullin comes out, I want you to watch where he goes. Don't challenge him and get yourself shot. Ain't no way I want to go back to Elkader and have to explain to your father why I let you get killed." He then turned to Tony, "You stay out front and I'll go into the house. If you hear shots and he comes out . . . kill him."

Karl saw worry on Josh's face and shock on Tony's. The younger brother was no longer hearing the words of his older brother Karl. He was getting orders from Captain August.

Leaving the horses behind the barn, the three men spread out to their planned positions. Karl gave Josh a few extra minutes to get around the house. Tony was standing at the corner of the building with his Navy Colt drawn. Karl was on the small porch, with his hand on the door latch. He nodded to Tony and then pushed the door open, disappearing inside.

There was the sound of shouting, then the crash of things being knocked over, then a woman screamed. A couple seconds later came the sound of a shot! Tony realized that it had come from the back of the house.

Knowing that he had been told to remain in front, he could not. Running around the back of the building, he saw Josh holding the Sharps rifle and looking toward the bank of the river. Karl came running out of the back door.

"He came at me, and I . . . I. It happened so fast. I just pointed and shot," the shaken Josh stammered. "He went down over the bank. I . . . I think I killed him."

With his gun ready, Karl went to the bank and looked. He put his Army Colt back into its holster. Sprawled on the riverbank lay Ray Scullin. Tony saw that a stern-faced old man had come out of the back door.

"What in the hell is going on here?" he growled. "You come busting into a man's house like that!" Then he paused for a moment. "Where's Ray?"

Tony watched his brother explain what had happened to the uncle. He could hear a woman crying inside the house. He went over to the riverbank. Ray wasn't wearing a gun, and Tony couldn't see any around him.

Walking back, Tony couldn't look at his friend. He couldn't tell him that he had shot an unarmed man. He mumbled, "I'll go get the horses."

They found the money in Ray's saddle bags. He had even kept the receipt that the purser had given Karl, eliminating any doubt that he had taken the money. After having the shock of someone bursting into his house wear off, the uncle admitted that Ray had been trouble since he'd been a young boy.

He had been a favorite of his wife, and the nephew's death would be tough on her. Karl and the uncle carried Ray's body to the barn and laid him in the feed room. The uncle said that he would bury his nephew in the morning.

The three men rode back to Sioux City in silence. Karl was weighing the thought of two lives for $500. Sid had shot him first, and that was a defense. He only wished that he had found a gun on Ray. During the war, Karl had seen soldiers advancing in battle and shooting one of their own, right in front of them. You can't hold a person responsible for mistakes during the heat of battle. If given the chance, Karl decided that he would try and explain that to Josh.

They arrived back at the grove of trees well after dark. Without much conversation, the horses were picketed and their gear was placed next to a cottonwood. Tony wanted some coffee and started a fire.

Karl sat by himself across from the fire and cleaned the Henry rifle, trying to get his mind off the shooting. He could hear Tony and Josh talk in low voices. It couldn't be too soon to get onto the steamboat and head for St. Louis, he thought. Their visit in Sioux City had not gone well. Karl was glad that the boys were talking.

They placed their blanket rolls just out of the light of the fire. The saddles were used for pillows, and hats kept the night dew off their heads.

Karl lay awake long after he heard the even breathing of the others. It was like during the war, he listened to the night. He half expected the sheriff to come looking for them. Finally, he fell into a restless sleep.

The sun was just about to come up. Karl had been lying under his warm covers, thinking about getting up.

"What's for breakfast?" Haat asked as he boldly walked into the camp. "Did I make enough noise?"

"I heard you coming a mile away," Karl lied. "I was just lying quiet so you could build the morning fire."

Seeing the Ho-Chunk seemed to raise the spirits of the three men. It was like the mood of last night had been broken.

They got out of their blankets and pulled their boots on after checking to make sure no critters had crawled into them. While they rolled up their bedrolls, Haat got the fire going and put on a pot of water for coffee.

Tony piped up, "Hey Haat, I thought you didn't like coffee."

Pouring some measured spoonful's of coffee into the water, Haat shot back, "I said I didn't like taste of coffee. I didn't say I did not know how to make."

Josh got out a blackened frying pan and began to slice salt pork into it. He had gotten a couple of boiled potatoes from the café the night before, and he sliced these into the crackling grease. Next, he brought out a loaf of bread that he also had gotten from the café.

Watching him with wonder, Tony asked, "What the heck did you tell that gal at the café? You got her whole pantry."

Josh smiled as he sliced the bread. "Just a few kind words about the meal, Tony, just a few kind words."

The coffee was good, and the bread dipped into salt pork grease with potatoes was most satisfying. Tony noticed that Haat had warmed a bit more water and made himself some tea with breakfast. He also saw that Haat had trimmed his hair just below the ear and was wearing a flat-brimmed leather hat. Tony told Haat that he liked the hat.

"I figured I better do something in case we are attacked on drive. I didn't want you confused about targets." The smile on his face let them know it was in good fun.

With the meal finished, the men quickly cleaned up and packed their gear. They decided to lead the horses to the dock. The hostler was coming out of the café and waved to them. Suddenly, he turned and hurried over to the men while tearing a chew off his tobacco plug.

"You folks mentioned that Ray Scullin might be in the area," he said, spitting a stream into the street. "I was talking about it to the sheriff this morning. He told me if I see you to tell you that he has a price on his head from a killing they think he done. Pays if he's dead or alive."

"We are about to board the boat," Karl replied. "If you could wait till we are downriver, then tell the sheriff to send the reward to his uncle. Ray was killed last night."

"Hot damn!" the man said. "I know a lot of folks that won't miss the cuss. I'll let him know."

Karl watched the old man hurry toward the livery. He glanced up at Josh, who was staring at the river as though he hadn't heard a word. Karl was thankful that the boy hadn't said anything to the hostler. He wouldn't have wanted to explain the circumstances of the shooting.

As they continued toward the boat, Haat asked, "What was that all about?"

"I'll tell you on some boring night when we are riding watch on the cattle," he replied. "Now, let's get these horses on the boat."

The steamboat from Sioux City to St. Louis was loaded and ready to leave promptly at 10 a.m. They were scheduled to arrive in St. Louis at noon the next day. There was one planned stop for passengers and to take on wood. Haat's friend waved at him and the Ho-Chunk said his good byes, taking the horses and heading for the stock ramp.

The passage included two meals. The meals were okay, but the coffee was weak. Karl, Tony, and Josh had a cramped room with four bunks. The extra bunk was used by a portly drummer who was working his way down to New Orleans. He sold patent medicines and tried his best to get the boys to buy some samples.

He followed them to the dining room, talking all the way about the benefits. Karl saw a table with three empty chairs and quickly steered the others to it. He apologized to the drummer because there were not enough seats. The drummer did not miss a beat, but walked over to another table and began to pitch them on the patent medicine, Kickapoo Elixir.

Tony struck up a conversation with a shapely brunette at the table. Once the meal was done, Karl went over to the lounge and took a stool at the bar. Josh and Tony had disappeared with the brunette and her promise of a friend.

Karl watched a card game next to him while he sipped a beer. He noticed that one player was a snappy dresser and supported a large ring on one finger. The rest of the men at the table looked like they worked for a living. No one seemed to be winning or losing too much money.

He saw that when it was the fancy dresser's turn to deal, it looked like something was wrong with the way he dealt the cards. Buying a second beer, Karl continued to watch the game. Sure enough, the fancy dresser was dealing off the bottom. Karl noticed that his winnings were building.

Karl stood and started to walk by when he pretended to trip and spilt his beer down the front of the fancy dresser. Angrily, the man jumped up and grabbed Karl's shirt.

"You clumsy son-of-a . . ." He stopped talking when he noticed that he was looking down the barrel of Karl's gun.

"These are good folks and they work hard for their money. They don't need you to cheat them out of it," Karl hissed. "Why don't you take the rest of the night off and give them a break?"

The fancy dresser released Karl and brushed the excess beer from this shirt. Karl heard him apologize to the table, saying that he had to go and change. Karl was leaning against the rail when the fancy dresser stomped by, swearing under his breath.

CHAPTER 7

There was a slow drizzle when they arrived in St. Louis. The captain gave several loud blasts of the steam whistle. He ran the steamboat against the pier. The crew tossed the lines to the waiting men. The gangway was slid out and immediately the waiting passengers began to push to get off the boat.

Karl and the others stood waiting under the second deck overhang. Those with horses were the last to get off. Haat came up and joined them. St. Louis had grown since their father had told them the stories. Today it was larger, but did not look like anything special. The heavy clouds and rain gave everything a gray, uninviting look.

After getting the horses off the boat, Haat said he wanted to spend the evening with his friends and would meet them in the morning. Watching the Ho-Chunk hurry off, Karl turned his attention to the horses. Selling them was easily done. They didn't even get away from the pier area before they got an offer they could not refuse. Happy with the top prices they had got, the group walked into town.

Karl marveled at the paved street. They saw a streetcar on rails, pulled by a tired-looking horse. They would have liked to ride on the street car, but it just did not make sense to pay when they could walk.

The first order of business was to find James and Albert. The plan had been to stay at one of the first hotels near the port. Karl noticed that there were several hotels. This could take time. They began to walk up the street, stopping at each hotel and asking if James Wolfe or Albert Keller were staying there.

They were just about to give up, and were quite wet from the rain, when they saw James sitting on a hotel porch with a fat cigar in his mouth. Josh yelled his name and ran to meet him. James was dressed in a store bought suit and looked quite the gentleman.

Karl walked up and shook his hand. "Good to see you, James. Do you know where Albert is?"

James shook his head. "I haven't seen him. I thought he may have caught up with you. I had to leave a week earlier than Albert on business for my father."

Karl went to the desk to inquire if they had heard from Albert and to see if any rooms were available.

"No, we haven't had an Albert Keller check in. I've got rooms, if you like. They are $10." Karl thanked him and walked back to the others.

"We got to look elsewhere. Albert's not here, and a room costs a third of a month's pay per night,"

Karl said with a disgusted look on his face. He then looked at James, realizing that he had been here for two weeks, paying that price. What a waste of money!

Tony and Josh pulled Karl aside. "Karl, we are supposed to meet the girls from the boat for a drink," Tony said. "Do you mind if we see them before we keep looking?"

Karl looked at the time on his pocket watch. "It is 2 p.m. now. Meet me back at the pier at 5 p.m. We need to find Albert, so I will keep looking. Keep your eyes open, in case he is around. I will also find a hotel we can afford to stay at."

"See you in the morning, Karl," James said as he walked back into the hotel.

Karl continued up the street, looking for a place where Albert might be staying. Passing by a policeman, he asked for any suggestions.

"Have you checked the hospital?" the officer asked. "Come to think of it, about a week ago a lad fresh off the steamboat got in a tangle with some of the thugs down there. I heard he was beat up pretty bad."

"I will do that," Karl replied, somewhat concerned. Before the policeman left, Karl asked about hotels.

Rubbing his chin, the officer said, "As far as a cheaper hotel, head south of town. You can find cheap rooms and the ladies can be a bargain." Laughing, the policeman turned and continued up the street.

Karl had passed the hospital down the street, so he walked back to make inquiries. Just inside the door he saw a woman behind the desk.

"Yes, we do have an Albert Keller. He was beaten and has some head injuries. You will find him straight back in room nine."

Karl rushed to the room. As he looked in, he couldn't help but gasp. There lay Albert with two blackened eyes, his head wrapped in bandages, and evidence of several bruises on his arms.

Karl rushed to the bed. "Albert, it's me, Karl. Do you know who I am?"

Albert slowly turned his head toward Karl. "I messed up, Karl. When I got off the boat, I asked a guy where I could find a hotel and he sent me into an alley. They were waiting for me and started hitting me. They took all my stuff and money. They tried to break one of my legs, but just bruised the heck out of it." Albert began to fade and doze off.

The doctor came into the room. "I heard someone had come in who knew Albert. He is going to be alright. He is groggy because we are giving him Laudanum for the pain."

Karl was relieved by the news. "When can he leave?"

The doctor looked at the chart near the bed. "He can leave anytime. Course, there is quite a bill he has run up that has to be paid first."

Karl glared at the doctor and thought, *Hold a man hostage until his bill is paid.* To the doctor he said, "I will be back in the morning to get Albert and pay the bill. Have him ready."

Patting Albert on the shoulder, he said, "We will be back to get you in the morning. Enjoy your rest here tonight. I am not sure your bed tomorrow will be as clean and comfortable."

Karl walked back to the pier to meet Tony and Josh. The sun was getting low in the sky and he was getting hungry. He had found a hotel that they could afford, just south of the center of town. The room had two double beds, and a stand with a pitcher of water. The outhouse was in back of the hotel. One door was for the ladies and the other for the men.

Karl noticed two rough-looking men walking toward him. He thought about the $500 in his money belt. In the open space of the pier, he felt somewhat safe. It was getting close to 5 pm and Tony and Josh would be here soon. That would help.

With his attention on the two thugs, Karl didn't notice a man slowly coming up behind him. He caught the movement just before the club hit his head. Karl attempted to duck, but not enough.

Dazed, he fell to the ground. The man behind him grabbed his vest from the back and started dragging him behind some large boxes of freight. Karl was able to see the other two running toward them.

Karl figured that the thug dragging him thought that he had a delivered a better hit on his head rather than a glancing blow. Karl let the thug drag him while trying to clear his head. Just behind the freight, he reached up, grabbed the man's coat and pulled him down, driving his bruised head into the thug's stomach. Fighting the throbbing in his skull, Karl then leapt to his feet. He caught the thug with a short jab on the end of his nose as he tried to straighten up. Grabbing the man's hair, he pulled the whiskered face down and brought his knee up to meet it.

The crunch told Karl that this would-be robber was done. Just then the other two rounded the corner of the freight box. They skidded to a stop, surprised to see Karl on his feet.

He snarled at them, "Your choice: Gutted with my knife, or gut shot." Karl was mad through and through.

Albert's beating may have been bad luck, but both of them being attacked wasn't an accident. Stepping forward with his gun in one hand and the knife in the other, Karl growled. The two thugs turned and ran.

Karl knelt near the one on the ground. He went through the pockets. He found a two-shot derringer, three $20 gold pieces, and a note. The note was written on hotel stationary and simply read: "5 pm main pier   sheepskin vest".

The man began to groan and Karl gave him another rap on the head with his gun barrel. Karl decided to keep the derringer and the money. He would let this thug pay for their stay in St. Louis. Stepping slowly from behind the freight, Karl checked for the other two before he walked out.

They were gone, but he saw Tony and Josh walking toward him.

Tony called out, "Sorry we are late, Karl. The ladies took forever to finish their drinks and then they asked us if we would escort them to their hotel. They asked us to wait while they used the bathroom first and then never came back."

Karl realized that that was the last piece of the trap. Suddenly, he felt cold inside. He looked closer at the piece of hotel stationary. While the hotel name was torn off, the trim was the same as he'd seen on the clerk's desk at James's hotel. James must have come down here early to set this up! While the hotel stationary was proof, it was not ironclad.

Karl could not be sure, but now he felt warned. Forewarned is prepared, he thought. He put the derringer into the inside pocket of his vest, the note into his money belt.

"I found Albert," Karl said. "He was beaten, but he'll be okay. How about we have a nice St. Louis meal before we go to the hotel?"

Tony rubbed his hands together. "Sounds like a great idea, maybe we will bump into the girls. Did you know you had blood on the side of your head?"

They picked Albert up from the hospital early the next morning. The bandage had been removed from his head, but his blackened eyes looked terrible. Carefully placing his hat onto his head, Albert limped from the hospital. The bill was $50. Their meal last night had been $8. With their room costing $2 dollars, Karl figured that they broke even in St. Louis.

Karl had asked the doctor to check his wound under the arm before leaving the hospital. It was scabbed over and itching. After a quick check, the doc had a nurse replaced the wrap around his ribs for support of the cracked rib. When asked what was owed, he told Karl that there was no charge. It raised his opinion of the doctor just a little.

Karl had let Haat know that they would be leaving on the 9 a.m. steamboat and would be getting off in Natchez, Mississippi. He also sent a note, using part of the hotel stationary to James, letting him know what steamboat they would be on. James met them on the pier with a curious look on his face.

"What happened to Albert?" James asked.

"He fell off that streetcar and damn near killed himself," Karl replied. Albert, with his bruised head and blackened eyes, simply nodded in agreement.

The steamboat was a little bigger than the last. They shared a room with eight other men. James had a stateroom and stayed alone. He offered to share with Josh, but Josh wanted to stick with Tony. It would take seven days to make the 600-mile trip. Karl was impressed with the short time. A direct route to Texas would have been almost a month by horseback. They would have been riding horses that cost over 5 times what horses could be bought for in Natchez.

They would still have two weeks of hard riding to their destination in Texas from Natchez. It would be late June before they could start rounding up cattle.

The meals were about the same, but the coffee was much better. Karl had confided in Tony about the trap set for them in St. Louis and the part that the girls appeared to play in it. He just wanted to warn Tony that if a girl was too easy to meet, go slow.

Karl would meet with Haat on the fantail each evening to talk. One night, Haat was excited. He had news about Texas.

"I have met a black man who knows where there are many cows," Haat said. "He was a slave before the war and worked on a ranch. The owner was killed during a Union raid on cattle. The cows now run loose."

Karl accepted a cup of tea that Haat brought him. He noticed that Haat was speaking better English. Using it every day was making a difference.

"Where are these cattle?" he asked Haat.

Haat blew on his cup of tea and took a sip. "He told me they are in Tyler, Texas. He said it is many days closer than Waco. He wants to go with us."

Karl smiled, looking at the large paddle churning the water behind the ship. "Tell him to be ready to move out right after we dock."

Thanking Haat, Karl was feeling pretty good and decided to treat himself to a shot and a beer. The lounge was crowded and smoke-filled. All the high rollers were there, looking for sheep to fleece. Karl found a stool at the end of the bar and ordered.

He looked around in amazement at the mirrors and shining brass trim everywhere in the room. The walls were tight-fitting boards rubbed to a high polish with wax. The bar was intricately carved with an ivory inlayed design.

Pretty girls were moving around the room, making sure that the players had drinks in their hands. They flirted to make tips from those who were winning.

The smiling bartender brought Karl his drinks. "That will be four bits. It's a busy night tonight. You should try your hand at the tables."

Shaking his head, Karl tossed some coins onto the bar. "I have many other ways to use my money, and it is too darn hard to come by."

Karl tasted the rye and then took a drink of the beer. He continued to watch the room. Suddenly, he picked out James at a table. He was playing with the fancy dresser. *There is justice*, he thought as he took another drink of the beer.

Karl was glad to see the piers of Natchez. Tony and Josh were enjoying shipboard life a bit too much. Each night they came in late, bragging of a good time. They had found a bar that catered to the working man and offered nickel beers. There were ladies to dance with and, for a bit more money, other things. Karl made sure that they didn't have money for other things.

James had been in a bad mood for several days. Karl was sure that it had something to do with the fancy dresser. Albert spent most of the trip resting from his ordeal in St. Louis.

Karl had talked with some freighters who knew Natchez well. It was an important trade route between the East and the Mississippi River. After the war, times had been tough. There were lots of freight wagons available at a good price.

Karl sat near their gear, watching the passengers disembark. All around him he could hear soft southern drawls. He felt tension in his spine. The war had ended about a year ago. At that time, Karl would have been in enemy territory. Being shot at, or expecting to be shot at, for four years had left a mark on him. Karl tried to shake the feeling off. He had to remember that the war was over. Was it ever over, he wondered?

He assigned Tony and Josh to get some supplies for the trip to Texas. He gave them a list and strict orders to buy nothing else, and to try to get the best prices. They had just over $850 left after expenses of the trip down. This included the money for delivering the horses, and what he had left Elkader with. He would owe each man at least $90 at the end of the drive. This could be paid out of the proceeds of the cattle sale.

Haat introduced Karl to Harold Washington. He was a tall, muscular, black gentleman. He looked every bit a cowboy.

In that slow southern drawl he said, "Ah appreciate you all taking me on."

"Glad to have you, Harold. Do you go by Harold or Harry?"

Smiling back at Karl, he said, "Harry is just okay by me."

Maybe Harry's smooth southern manner would be good therapy, Karl thought. James was in a hurry to get moving, so they picked a place to meet. Tony and Josh headed for town, while Haat and Harry said that they would check out some horses to pull a freight wagon.

Karl had read about the chuck wagon that was developed by Charles Goodnight. It was said that he'd used a converted Army wagon. Karl figured that a freight wagon with heavy axles should work well. He could make it into a chuck wagon. In the meantime, they could all ride west in the wagon. Cow ponies would be more plentiful in Texas. Karl made sure that James stayed with him. He didn't want him to set up any more surprises. Albert stayed on the pier to watch their gear.

They found a wagon in excellent shape for the unbelievable price of $10. Haat and Harry found a freighter who was getting out of the business and selling his stock. They were able to get four horses and harnesses for $110. By the time that Tony and Josh returned, carrying two heavy bags of supplies each, the wagon was waiting, loaded with their saddles, bedrolls, saddle bags, and rifles.

James was going to purchase a riding horse in Natchez, but changed his mind after seeing the wagon. It had low sides and canvas, resembling a covered wagon. Karl would have to build a box on the back for the cook. The gate would be designed to fold down with two legs, making a surface to prepare food on.

It was late afternoon when they pulled out for Texas. Harry was singing a slow southern song about going home. The date was June 21, 1866.

CHAPTER 8

They only drove for two hours the first day. Karl wanted to make sure that the wagon worked well. The axles had been freshly lubricated, and the harnesses were in good repair. Karl noticed that the hand brake linkage, which was a heavy leather strap, needed to be shortened a bit.

There was enough room for all six in the wagon. Karl and Albert sat in front, with Karl handling the reins. Haat walked alongside with his bow, keeping an eye out for fresh meat for supper. Haat also had an older cap and ball pistol, which he stored in the wagon. The saddles were lined along the side and used for seats. Bed rolls were stacked to the front. James had a bottle and took a drink every so often.

Once away from town, Karl started looking for someplace to spend the night. They found a good location for the first night, near a clear running stream. They were in Louisiana. It was hot and humid, which was typical of June.

The sun went down in a blaze of red. Clouds of mosquitoes came out, looking to suck the blood out of them. Karl had forgotten how humid it was in the South. Arkansas had been hot and sticky enough during the war. This was even farther south. Despite the warm night, they slept with their blankets over their heads, for protection from the biting insects.

Harry mixed up a concoction with a horrendous odor that he said would keep mosquitoes away. They rubbed it on, and he was right, but the smell would also keep anyone else they should meet away. Karl rubbed some onto the horses to give them protection.

Louisiana was green and wet. Biscuits would mold in a day from the heat and moisture. It rained every day. Karl found that he liked the variety of wild life. Large flocks of ducks would rise out of a pond as they approached. No doubt the smell drove them away, he figured. White birds with curved bills were everywhere. The woods and swamps were full of noises from the songs of birds and the chorus of frogs. He saw flowers growing right up into the trees.

They ate well, supplementing their food by hunting. Haat continued to walk rather than ride. He said that it kept him as one with the earth. He kept them in meat and scouted ahead for any danger. There was always the possibility of holdouts from the war attacking travelers. Karl felt comfortable with the number of guns that they had available. Marauding outlaws usually looked for soft targets.

There were no signs saying "Welcome to Texas", but Karl was sure that they were there when things began to dry up and he saw doves flying by in the evening. They stopped in Marshall for supplies. Harry said that it wasn't a good place for him. He stayed by the wagon with Albert while the rest of them went into town for supplies.

Marshall had had a concentration of slaves before the Civil War, until the Union Army took it over in June 1865. A year later, the town was still much divided over the issue. They purchased things that were needed and quietly left town.

It was now only three days to Tyler. One of the horses began to favor a front leg. Karl stopped near a grove of chestnut trees.

"We can spend the night here," he said. "I need to check on the horse."

James climbed off the wagon and sat under the trees with his bottle. Karl checked the horse. A stone had lodged in the hoof. He pried it out with his knife. The shoe was a little loose and would require fixing. He decided to have two horses pull the wagon and tie the others to the back until they came across someplace to have the shoe repaired.

James came over and looked at the horse. "It ain't too bad. I say we pull with four horses."

Karl turned to James. "If the hoof is damaged pulling the wagon, we end up losing a horse."

James scowled, looking at Karl. "It is just a damn horse. If it goes bad, we shoot it and get another."

Now, Karl wasn't attached to the horse in any way, but he did not believe in wasting horse flesh. "I don't agree, James. We . . ."

The punch came out of nowhere, catching Karl on the side of the head. Lights flashed in his skull and he fell under the horses. With the animals startled, Karl crawled to the other side, avoiding the hoofs and shaking his head.

Falling under the horses had given him the time that he needed to focus his eyes before James had a chance to charge. James's face was wild as he came around the horses after Karl.

"What the hell is the matter with you, James? Did you get bad liquor or what?"

Growling, James grabbed for Karl. He was coming in for the squeeze. Karl side stepped and elbowed James in the kidneys as he went by.

James turned around, his arms wide spread. Karl did not wait. He stepped in, leading with a right to James's midsection, and then ducked under his grasp. He followed up with a left behind his ear.

The two turned to each other and began to trade punches. James landed a solid punch on the corner of Karl's eye that split the skin. Karl flattened James's nose with a right. They clinched and James got his arms around Karl's' waist, then began to squeeze. Karl felt his breath go out and a sharp pain in his back.

In desperation, he head-butted James, doing additional damage to his nose. Then he hooked his heel around James's leg, sending them both to the dusty road. The impact broke the grip and Karl planted both feet on James's chest and shoved as hard as he could. James flew back against the wagon wheel, striking his head on the hub.

Dazed, he sat there with blood flowing out of his nose, splattering the front of his shirt. Karl slowly got up, breathing heavily, with blood running down his face from the cut along his eye. The fight was over without a real winner.

Josh came over and helped his brother up and handed him a rag for his nose.

Tony stood looking at Karl. "What the heck was that all about?" he asked.

Karl watched Josh help James to the shade. "It's nothing, Tony, just a disagreement about a horse."

With two horses pulling the wagon and the other two tied to the back of the wagon, they continued toward Tyler. Haat and Harry walked to take some weight off the wagon. James slumped in the bottom of the wagon, sleeping off what he had been drinking.

Albert looked over at Karl. "That eye is going to match mine. He clipped you a good one. Here, let me drive for a while."

Karl was glad to let Albert have the reins. His head was aching from the punches that had landed. He was not sure what to do about James. They needed the horses that he was supposed to buy, and he was sure that if he sent him away, he would leave with the horse money. Just maybe that was his plan. Nothing was easy.

Harry directed them to a ranch that he knew would have cow ponies. Acting as though nothing had happened, James joined Karl to select horses. James's nose was broken, and both of his eyes were blackened. Karl had a nice shiner on the right side. He also had several tender spots, and the fight hadn't done his ribs any good.

They spent the afternoon haggling with the rancher, who had a surplus of horses and little money. While the group did not have a lot, what cash they had looked very attractive to him. They finally settled on $15 per horse. James had enough money to purchase 30 horses. It was not as many as Karl felt that they needed, but he had evidently wasted and gambled away much of the money given to him for horses.

Harry was great with the horses and was dubbed the wrangler for the drive. He personally checked each of the horses as they were purchased. Most were mustang mix and had worked around cattle. The rancher had a decent blacksmith shop, so Karl fixed the lose shoe and checked the rest of the team. For $3 the rancher sold Karl tools and nails, so that they could fix any future problems.

Two days later, Harry pointed to an abandoned ranch house. "There she is, Mista Karl. That's the place. Back about two miles, there is a canyon with plenty of water and grass to collect the cattle. We can build a fence out of mesquite to close off the open end. One side has a lot of catsclaw, which makes a natural barrier."

Karl had asked Harry not to call him Mista, but Harry insisted. He had said, "When you like and respect a man, it is only right to call him Mista."

Karl looked around the ranch. He saw several cattle grazing in the noon sun and he could see groves of pecans. Some alder indicated the location of water. There were several magnolia trees around the house. It was hard to believe that someone had not taken over the ranch.

James made himself at home in the ranch house, choosing the large bedroom. The single-story building had four rooms. It had a main living and dining area, a kitchen, and two bedrooms. Everything was covered with dust and would require some cleaning.

Karl offered to share a bedroom with Tony. He had seen the bunkhouse and decided that a real cowboy slept in there. The rest of the men grabbed their gear and followed Tony to the bunkhouse.

There was a low barn with a large sagging door. Karl found a little hay inside and a good-sized corral which needed some repair. Karl checked the well. It would need to be cleaned, but it promised water that was cold and clear.

If he didn't have to get cattle to Kansas, he was sure that this would make a fine place to raise a family. The family would include a good-looking redhead. Karl had thought about Karen a lot since spending time with her. If nothing else was certain, he was sure that they would meet again.

Karl set up a schedule for the roundup. They would need to spend at least two days cleaning and repairing stuff they needed. Tony and Josh were assigned to constructing a brush fence in the canyon. Haat and Harry were to scout the range, looking for cattle.

The plan was to round up the easiest cattle before they worked the more difficult areas. Albert would work on the corral and barn. Karl decided to clean the well himself. James was nowhere to be found. It was evident that he had gotten up early and, taking one of the horses, had headed for Tyler.

Karl gave the house a cursory cleaning and then worked on the well. Finishing, he put together a noonday meal for everyone. After eating, he went over to the pasture where they were keeping the horses.

Karl spent the next three hours working kinks out of some of the horses. Finally, he selected a three-year-old buckskin that he liked and decided that it would be his personal horse. The buckskin took the bit without any problem. Karl noticed that it pulled in air when he tightened the cinch. After waiting a moment, the horse relaxed and he retightened the cinch.

He could see some hills to the southwest, and decided that it would be a good vantage point to survey the area. Letting Albert know where he was going, Karl turned the horse toward the hills.

The buckskin was a pleasure to ride with its smooth gait. The warm sunshine and fresh air made it great to be alive. It took about an hour to reach the hills. Karl walked the horse up the slope, choosing an old trail that had probably been used by wild horses or deer.

He could see Tony and Josh working on the fence. The progress was good, and they should be able to finish with one more day. He could see smoke drifting up from the ranch house. Albert must be starting supper. To the northwest he could see a slow-moving rider. He guessed that it would be James coming back.

Karl rode down the hill toward Tony and Josh. Riding up to the boys, he swung out of the saddle. Just as he stepped to the ground, his horse side-stepped and snorted. Karl then heard the rattles. Within two feet of his boot was a snake, ready to strike.

"Don't move, Karl!" It was Tony, and he took a couple steps around Karl.

His arm flashed, sending the Good Knife into the snake just behind the head. The knife pinned it to the ground and the dying body coiled and uncoiled around the handle.

Karl stepped away from the snake and calmed the buckskin. "Nice throw, brother. What would you have done if you had missed?"

Laughing, Tony pulled the knife out of the snake and wiped the blade in the sand. "I'll let you know if I ever do."

Supper was ready when they got back. James had returned drunk and was snoring loudly in his room. Albert had beans and biscuits, with strong coffee to wash them down.

Haat and Harry came in after dark. "Mista Karl, we counted about 400 to 500 head of stock east of here. Should only take a short time to round them up. Tomorrow, we will check south. You know, many of the older ones have the Leaning J brand on them. You may want to go into town and register it and another for yourself. Be a shame if we got them all rounded up and someone else went in and registered the brand."

Karl nodded. "I'll go into town in the morning. We'll need a road brand for the drive. How about the Circle A, for Oli August?"

They all raised their cups. "To the Circle A." Albert asked to ride into Tyler with Karl. He had a letter that he wanted to mail to Jenny.

The morning was cool when they rode out for Tyler. One could see the horses' breath as they snorted. Tony and Josh had selected a couple of horses and had them saddled and ready. They figured that the canyon would be ready for cows the next day. James had mumbled something about checking west of the ranch for cattle. Haat and Harry were gone before daylight, checking south.

Albert made small talk during the ride to Tyler. He told Karl about plans that he and Jenny had made. He kidded Karl about Karen at the fort. In less than 45 minutes, they rode into Tyler.

The town was bigger than Karl had expected. The first order of business was to register the brands. They found the small brick building next to the jail that they were directed to. There they could register brands.

Karl looked around the small office. There was paper everywhere. The portly clerk behind the desk set his pipe down as they walked in.

"Can I help y'all with something?" the clerk drawled. The man smelled of garlic.

Karl handed him a piece of paper with the two brands sketched on them. "We need to register a couple brands."

The clerk looked at the paper as he mopped his sweating brow with a stained cloth. He looked up at Karl. "I certainly can help you with the one brand, but the Leaning J is registered."

Karl's face showed his surprise. "I understood that when a ranch was abandoned, an interested party could take the brand over."

Nodding, the clerk agreed. "You're right, but that has already been done."

"I didn't realize that." Karl knew that it would be a setback, but they could still brand the mavericks.

"Yes sir, a guy came in yesterday and registered it," said the clerk as he shuffled through some papers, looking for the correct form for Karl.

"Yesterday!" Karl exclaimed.

"A stocky fellow with a moustache came yesterday and registered it," the clerk continued. "Kind of surprising, though. Old man Jones been dead for four years, with no kin. Suddenly, two of y'all come in to register his stock. Course, it is legal to do so. First come, first serve."

Karl was shocked. He looked down at the registry paper that the clerk showed him and it had the name of James Wolfe.

"That son-of-a . . ." Karl stifled the rest of the curse. "He knew damn well I was coming here today to register the brand. While we all worked yesterday, he came in and blindsided us."

Karl's face was red and his eyes blazing. He had never wanted to hurt anyone before, but he sure wanted to do so now.

Albert grabbed his shoulder. "Karl, listen to me. There are lots of unbranded cattle out there. In fact, most are mavericks. We will register the Circle A and concentrate on building a herd. It is no more work driving some of Wolfe's cow's north than just yours. We will make sure that he doesn't brand any more with the Leaning J."

Karl's blood was boiling, but Albert was right. Most of the cattle were mavericks. Karl filled out the form for the clerk, registering the Circle A brand.

"That will be a dollar for the registration fee," the clerk said, holding out his hand.

Before they left town, Karl picked up chaps for everyone and some extra rope. There was not much talk on the ride back to the ranch. Supper was on the stove when they walked in. Big beef steaks were frying in a large iron skillet.

Harry looked over at the two. "Haat and I decided we needed some beef to eat before we start working the cattle, Mista Karl."

The frying beef smelled good. "Was it branded or unbranded?" Karl asked.

"Branded Leaning J, Mista Karl," Harry said.

"Good!" Karl replied.

The sun was setting in the western sky, streaks of red clouds making it a beautiful night. Karl had not mentioned anything about the registration during supper. He was sitting on the porch with a cigar when James came out. He seemed in good spirits.

"Saw you registered the Leaning J brand," Karl said, taking a long drag on the cigar.

"I sure did. I figured one of us should before we started rounding up cattle," James said with a self-satisfied look on his face. "Didn't make any sense us rounding up all them cows and someone else making claim."

Controlling what he really wanted to say, Karl continued, "We will be branding all the mavericks Circle A. If I see any fresh brands with Leaning J, it would be mighty hard to explain."

James sat with his jaws clenched, staring at the sunset. Karl figured that he had said enough. Nothing would be gained by fighting and injuring one another just before starting roundup. Shortly after, James went into the house and re-emerged with a bottle. He walked toward the pecan grove grumbling something that Karl could not understand.

It was morning, and the first day of the roundup. The sky was clear and the sun was bright in the morning sky. Karl stepped out onto the porch and stopped short. In front of him was a short-stooped old Mexican who had a long, white, tobacco-stained beard. Karl stepped back in surprise.

"I heard you were looking for a cook, Señor," the old Mexican said.

Surprised, Karl responded, "Your name wouldn't be Jose, would it? My father told me stories of a cook by that name."

Smiling, with his yellow teeth showing, the Mexican shook his head. "No Señor, my name is Poco. It stands for *little*. If you want, I can be Jose."

Karl smiled back at the little man. "No, Poco is fine. We are heading out to start the roundup. You have supper ready just before dark. We will decide then. You will find supplies in the kitchen and a quarter of beef under netting down in the root cellar."

Poco pointed to the wagon. "Is that going to be the chuck wagon?"

Karl nodded. He heard Tony calling to him to hurry up. The boy was anxious to start cowboying. "See you this evening," Karl said, and headed toward his saddled buckskin.

They split up into two groups. Tony, Josh, and Harry worked toward the southeast. Karl, James, Albert, and Haat worked east and northeast. The cattle were plentiful.

Their horses turned out to be well-trained for the job of rounding up cattle. Karl hazed three cows out of some mesquite with his coiled rope. His cows were joined by six animals driven by Haat. They drove them to the canyon and headed back to look for more.

Soon, a routine was set up. Albert and Haat pushed the cattle out while Karl and James moved them into the canyon. They seemed content to be in the grassy canyon, so they didn't have to close the opening each time. The other group came up with a similar plan. Tony and Josh pushed the cattle out and Harry drove them to the canyon.

Most of the cattle were willing to be driven. Some of the wilder ones would break away, but the buckskin was quick and cut them off, pushing them back to the bunch. The first time that the buckskin went after a cow, Karl was almost unseated. The horse was quick. After that, Karl anticipated the moves and enjoyed how a good cow pony worked.

By the noon break they had 70 or more cattle in the canyon. Extra horses had been brought to the canyon mouth and were tied under some oaks. Karl noticed a table set up near the horses. There was a bucket of cold water with a dipper, a plate of sliced beef and a basket of biscuits under a towel. A bowl was filled with a type of sauce made from chili peppers that Karl did not recognize, but it made the beef taste great.

Everyone sat on the ground near the table and wolfed down the meal. Tony and Josh were talking about the cattle they had found. Karl liked the fact that their eyes were dancing with excitement as they talked. He knew that after a few more days exhaustion would set in and some of the fun would be gone.

Poco passed the first test with the meal. It was getting dark when they returned to the ranch house. Poco yelled out the door, "Wash your hands, and come and get it!" Karl was turning his horse loose in the corral when he noticed that the wagon was halfway into the barn.

Walking around the wagon, he saw that Poco had been busy converting it into a chuck wagon. The box in the back was done and it had a tailgate for preparing meals. He had wood cut out for shelves that had not been installed yet.

Walking into the ranch house, Karl saw an impressive spread on the table. There was beef, beans, some kind of greens, some kind of pie with pecans, and a hot pot of coffee on the stove. Hungry from a hard day's work, they dug in without any conversation.

Karl looked at Poco, who was standing expectantly near the stove. "You're hired."

Around the table there was a chorus of, "Yeah!"

The first week was very productive. They had over 400 head in the canyon. About 300 of them had to be branded with Circle A and any bulls were castrated. Full days were set aside for branding. Dust, sweat, and the smell of burning hair filled the air. Harry spent time showing everyone proper techniques of roping and tying the cattle for branding. James did the castrating, tossing the testicles into a wooden bucket.

Poco came down one day and took a good portion of the testicles from the bucket. That night he had them fried up, along with beef steak, for supper. There was a lot of kidding about who would try them first.

Josh picked one up and toasted his brother with it. "James, I am honored to try the results of your work."

After a bit, everyone but James tried them and agreed that they weren't bad. No doubt James was too close to the production to eat one.

Then the rains came. It was steady and cool. James said that he had left his knife at the branding station and offered to check on the cattle while he went and got it. When he came back he said that all was okay. He then went into his room and opened a bottle.

Karl kept busy repairing and setting up things for the drive. Poco had made three drives before. He had missed this spring's drive because of a broken leg. Karl knew how important the cook was. He moved ahead of the herd, picking out a good place to spend the night and get supper ready by the time that the herd arrived.

After three days, the rain stopped. The wind was cool, so Karl put his old wool Union coat on. He had kept it because it was warm and easy to move in. All the military rank had been removed. Grabbing his flat-brimmed hat, he strode over to the corral. The horses stomped and snorted, moving to the far side. Karl deftly dropped a loop on the buckskin.

The sky was still overcast, with low hanging clouds that sprinkled a little rain. Karl rode up to check on the cattle. In just a few days of rain, the plants had responded and the pastures had hints of new green growth. There were no puddles of standing water. The thirsty ground had sucked it up.

Karl pulled his horse up sharply at the canyon. There was a large hole in the brush fence. He knew that there had been wind during the storm. Maybe it had blown the brush apart. A quick check proved that about half the cattle had wandered out.

Karl sat under the oak tree, tossing acorns at the table, while staring at the hole. James may have opened the fence, but he had no proof. James worked as hard as anyone when they were rounding up cattle, especially branding. It didn't make sense opening the fence to let them out. Karl decided that from now on he would make sure that he always knew where James was.

Karl heard two horses walking slowly up behind him. He turned, expecting to see some of the crew. Two whiskered and somewhat shabby men looked down at him. One, with a thick neck, had a rifle across his saddle. While it was not aimed at Karl, it would not take much of a move to do so. The other had a poorly-fixed broken nose.

"Whatcha doin' with our cows?" the broken nose man asked.

Karl looked at the man who spoke. The man sat with his coat open and his hand resting near his Navy Colt. Both men were wearing Confederate pants. Slowly, Karl turned to face the men as he came to his feet.

He forced a smile onto his face. "Howdy, gents. I am afraid you are mistaken. These were mavericks that we branded."

Trying to throw them off their plan, Karl continued. "Look at the fence, somehow it got open and we lost half of the cows. You didn't happen to see some?"

By this time Karl had his coat open and his hand on his hip, inches away from the Army Colt. The man with the thick neck noticed the move and turned his horse slightly to bring the rifle to bear on Karl.

"He said they were our cows. No Union scum is coming . . ."

Karl saw the rifle coming up and threw himself to the side. He felt something slam his right side, followed by the report of the rifle.

Karl was back in army mode. More than once he had been confronted by what appeared to be a no-win situation, and by moving quickly, without hesitation, he had changed the odds to his favor.

Karl's right leg gave way and he tried to roll as he fell. Another bullet hit the dirt beside him. When Karl rolled back to face the men, he was bringing up his Army Colt. His first shot struck the neck of the horse of the man with the rifle. He had been aiming at the man's chest, but the horse had been turned between them.

The animal reared back, blood spraying from the artery. It fell, hitting against the other man's horse. Both men crashed to the ground. Karl rolled behind the oak. One horse was down, kicking and dying, and the other ran a short distance away.

Karl shot at the man with the thick neck as he scrambled to get behind the downed horse. The bullet went through the man's leg. Karl could see the man with the broken nose lying on the ground where he'd fallen. He was struggling to get up. A bullet hit the tree trunk, sending bark flying into Karl's face.

He heard the man lying on the ground. "Help me Ed, my legs don't work! Ed!"

Karl watched as the man named Ed swung his rifle and shot his partner. He then abandoned the fight, ducking between trees and limping toward the loose horse.

Karl stood up, supporting himself with the tree. He shouted, "Stop! Don't make me kill you!"

Ed turned to fire at Karl. Karl shot twice, putting two bullets into Ed's chest. Ed dropped his gun and sank to his knees. He reached for the weapon with a shaky hand before collapsing on top of it. Karl felt his heart pounding as he slowly headed for the two men. He could feel blood running down his side. His leg was tingling.

He looked at the two men. Frustrated, anger welled through Karl. "The damn war is over. I don't want to kill anymore."

The adrenalin drained from Karl and he suddenly felt light-headed. He grabbed for a tree, missed and fell. He lay on the ground, looking at the overcast sky.

Karl wasn't sure how long he had lain there before he recognized the voices of his crew coming toward him.

"What the hell!" he heard Tony say.

Running up to his brother, Tony lifted Karl's head. "Are you okay? Where are you hit?"

Karl looked at Tony's worried face. "I'll be okay. Just my side."

Tony checked the wound. "The bullet cut across your hip, Karl. You have an awful crease, but it doesn't look too deep."

Karl figured that the impact temporarily numbed his leg. Tony and Albert helped him to his feet. Karl sat against the table and watched as Haat started a fire to heat water and make a poultice to cover the wound.

"We lost some cattle, Haat," Karl said.

Haat continued to work on the poultice as he answered. "Someone pulled it open. I found where the brush had been dragged, not rolled by wind. The rain didn't wash out all of sign."

"That is what I suspected."

Tony and Josh came back from closing up the fence. "Half the cattle are gone," Josh said. "Harry is looking to see if any of them bunched up someplace close."

While Haat cleaned the wound and applied the poultice and bandage, Karl told them about the two men. As he told them the story, he could see James walking around the two men. He shoved each with his foot to make sure that they were dead.

"Why did you shoot the horse, Karl?" Tony asked.

"I was shooting at the man. Damn shame he pulled the horse over and put its head between me and him. It's an awful waste of horse flesh," Karl said, shaking his head.

Karl and Albert took the two bodies into Tyler tied across the broken nose man's horse. Sheriff Benson looked the two men over.

"You say Ed here shot Andy after he was knocked off his horse. Ed never did have any spine," the sheriff said. "Sorry boys, it's out of my jurisdiction. Y'all got to go up the street and talk to the military folks. What these boys did was an act of war, by what you said. They gotta take care of it."

It took most of the day before they got rid of Ed and Andy. Karl decided that during the rest of the stay in Texas, he would keep his Union coat out of sight. There were still a lot of mixed feelings in Texas.

They worked steadily until the end of July. Karl's hip healed quickly. He would have to ask Haat what was in the poultice someday. Karl had hired two more men from Tyler who were looking for a drive north.

Albert came back from Tyler after purchasing last minute supplies for the drive. Karl was taking a break and enjoying some lunch put out by Poco. Albert was galloping his horse and waving an envelope.

"It's a letter from Karen!" he shouted. "I also got one from Jenny!"

Pulling up, Albert handed Karen's letter to Karl. He looked at the smooth flowing hand writing on the envelope. He tucked it into his vest pocket. He wanted to read the letter later, when he was alone.

Albert read his letter to everyone at supper. It contained news from home. Karl sat alone near the corral and enjoyed Karen's letter. She had gotten the one he'd sent. Her words of endearment tore at his heart.

Working hard, one forgets that loved ones and home are far away. A letter can be a painful reminder. Yet the promise of love can give a man strength to finish the job.

"You going to share your letter too?" Tony kidded as he forked hay to the horses.

Karl barely heard him. He was reading the letter for the third time.

They had just over 800 head in the canyon and would have to move the cattle soon. The grass was getting sparse. Another week and there would be nothing left. One of the new hires named John had a suggestion

"You know, Karl," he said, "there is a ranch north of Tyler, owned by a man named Wooden, that is quickly going under. My guess is you could buy some cows for as little as $3 each."

Karl figured that it would be worth a try. He asked Haat to keep an eye on James. Haat nodded without question. Karl asked Albert to join him. With the morning sun at their backs, they rode toward the ranch.

It was a small, hardly-can-make-it spread. A tired-looking man in wool pants and suspenders walked toward them. He had no shirt on, just his long johns top, which was sweat and dirt-stained around the top. Rolling the chew in his cheek, he looked Karl and Albert over.

"What can I do you fer?" he asked.

Karl wished that he was upwind of the man. "My name is Karl August and this here is Albert Keller. If you're Mr. Wooden, I hear you have some cows you might be willing to sell."

Karl noticed a woman in a faded dress standing in the doorway of the house. Two dirty-faced young kids clung to her dress.

"I be Hal Wooden," the man said while he thought for a minute. "Wal, I got some yonder. Maybe 400 head. I wanted to drive them to market, but I got no hands left."

Karl asked to see the cattle. Hal went to the barn and brought out a good-looking chestnut mare. Throwing a saddle onto the mare, he swung aboard with the most graceful moves Karl had ever seen. The three rode a mile west of the ranch. Karl looked at the herd. The cattle were in good shape. They were mature and needed to be driven to market.

"I am looking for only 200 head. I will pay you $3 a head." Karl felt comfortable because Hal had no bargaining position.

Spitting a stream of brown tobacco juice, Hal rubbed his chin. "I have never sold cattle for so little. Course, the others won't be worth nothing being left here. I tell you what. I will sell you 200 head for $2 each. If you take all 400 and when y'all sell em, send me the money for my 200."

"There will be losses on the trail." Karl said.

Hal spit again. "Yep, that I know. That's why you're getting the others for $2."

They rode back toward the ranch. Karl hadn't said yes or no. He saw the man's wife hanging laundry on the line while the little ones dragged her basket. Here was a family that was working hard.

The war had left them in a bad way. Just maybe a little help would keep those youngsters fed.

"Okay, Mr. Wooden. We'll be driving our herd by here in the next couple of days. Have your cattle ready. I'll bring your money."

As they rode back to their ranch, Karl had a good feeling about the deal. He really could not afford the $400 for the cattle. It would leave him short. But they had no more time to spend driving cattle out of the breaks at the rate of 8 to 12 a day. He had a cook, a wrangler, a scout, and seven others, including himself, to drive the cattle. It just might work, God willing.

CHAPTER 9

The final tally was 1,238 longhorns to drive north. The Leaning J brand was on 160 of the cattle. At some point, Karl would have to take up the registration issue with James. When they got to market would be soon enough.

It was daybreak as they moved away from Hal Wooden's ranch. A mossy old steer with one broken horn took the lead. The plan was to drive the cattle late into the evening, to put enough miles behind them so that they wouldn't be tempted to turn back. Karl started at drag and spent the day eating dust. He felt that everyone should take turns in each position around the herd. Starting off at drag would show the others that nobody was above a position.

The sky was bright blue. The day would be hot. The drive would take about two months. They would encounter several hazards: Rivers, storms, snakes, herd cutters, Indians trying to steal horses, and lack of grazing or water. When summed up, driving a herd made little sense. But if successful, the payoff was good.

Haat ranged out in front, looking out for trouble and supporting Poco. One never knew when the chuck wagon might become a target for raiders looking for food. They were heading for the Chisholm Trail, which went through Oklahoma. They would meet up with it after crossing the Red River.

The grazing across Texas would be marginal. The cattle pulled the bean pods off the mesquite bushes every chance that they had. Water would not be a problem, due to rains that had come in when two tropical storms came ashore near Galveston.

Mel, the other man whom Karl had hired, came to the back to relieve him. Karl rode up a knoll alongside the herd and pulled out some jerky and a biscuit. It was impressive to see the herd of longhorns moving through the valley. They were spread out in a long line extending about a half-mile.

Toward the evening stop, they would have to start bunching the herd. The process took up to an hour. Taking a drink from his canteen, Karl rode to get a fresh horse. Harry had one roped and ready to have the saddle switched to it. He then rode to the left flank to relieve Tony.

He shouted to his brother, "Are we having fun?"

"You darn right we are!" Tony yelled back.

Two hours before dark Karl saw the chuck wagon parked and set up for supper. Paco had a fire going and a large pot hanging over the flames. It was time to start bunching the herd. Haat came over to help him turn the lead animals. Slowly, the herd came to a stop and the cattle began to range out and graze.

Karl had Mel and John stay with the herd while the rest of the men went to get ready for supper. A shallow stream ran past the chuck wagon and emptied into a pond. By the time that the trail dust had been washed off, Poco was calling them to eat.

The men were divided into four groups of two for riding night herd. It would be Mel and John, Harry and Haat, Josh and Tony, and James and Karl. Each would take a three-hour shift. Karl figured that they would drive the herd 10 to 12 hours each day.

When they reached better grazing, they would give the cattle more time to graze and the day's drive would be shorter. After eating the beans and biscuits Poco served, Karl sat with the ledger, making notes about the herd and the conditions of the drive. Tony came over with two tin mugs of coffee.

"Poco just made a fresh pot. I figured you might like one," he said, handing his brother a mug.

"Thanks, Tony," Karl said, tasting the coffee. "I have a good feeling about the drive. We got a healthy herd out there. I would have liked a couple more hands and more horses, but if we're careful and have some luck, we'll be back in Elkader with the money with time to spare."

"Haat noticed some riders shadowing us," Tony informed Karl. "He guessed there were four."

"We can expect some of that," his brother replied. "Lot of folks are curious when a large herd moves through. Some worry that the cattle will be driven on their grazing. Some may be watching for a stray to take down and feed the family."

"I figured I should let you know," Tony said. Finishing his coffee, he headed for his bedroll to catch a couple hours sleep before his watch.

While Karl made light of the riders, he knew that they could also be trouble. Even though the cattle weren't worth much in Texas, there were those who didn't think outsiders should be able to come in and drive them out.

They were still several days from the Red River. Once across the river, issues of who should have the cattle would be gone, but other problems would face them. Karl didn't want to put three-man shifts on to watch the cattle at night, but if those shadowing them stayed on, he would be forced to.

Later that night, Karl was woken by Haat for his watch. Pulling his boots on, he went to wake James. Karl could smell the whiskey on him. Harry had two horses saddled for them. Climbing onto his animal, James rode toward the far side of the herd, singing some off-tune song.

"Everything quiet, Harry?" Karl asked the wrangler.

"Haat caught sight of a fire earlier," he replied. "Otherwise, it's been a quiet night."

Karl climbed onto the mustang and sat, one leg crossed over the horn. He pulled a cigar out of his shirt pocket. Striking a match on the heel of his boot, he lit the stogie. It was two in the morning and all was quiet. Swinging his leg back, he stuck his boot into the stirrup and rode slowly around the herd, watching the horizon for any sign of another camp.

Poco outdid himself the next morning. He had made biscuits the night before and served a pot of white gravy with pieces of beef for breakfast. Tony and Josh were riding herd when the men were called to eat.

Karl and Harry finished first and went to the herd to relieve the boys so they could eat. As the men finished their meal, they headed for the remuda to catch and saddle a horse to start the day.

Shouting and waving their lariats the cowboys started the herd moving. Once the cattle were strung out for travel, Harry brought the extra horses up and kept them on the upwind side.

Poco remained alone, cleaning up after breakfast. Once done, he would easily overtake the cattle and move ahead. At midday he would let them catch up and have something that the men could take and eat while riding. He would then move ahead, looking for a good spot to stop the herd for the night and then start the supper.

This same routine would play out each day of the drive. The weather remained good, making the cattle easier to handle. The fourth day out, Karl saw the chuck wagon set up next to a pond. There were riders stopped around the wagon.

Karl told John to alert the rest of the men of possible trouble. He took the loop off his Army Colt and rode toward the chuck wagon. There were two men mounted along the side of the wagon and two others on the ground, talking to Poco. They turned to look when Karl rode up.

While none of the men had a gun showing, they all appeared to be ready for immediate action. Stopping short of the wagon, Karl asked, "Is there something I can do for you boys?"

One of the men on the ground smiled and rubbed his whisker-covered chin. Flipping his coat open, he displayed a badge. "We come from Tyler looking for some cows that were rustled. We need to check your herd and papers."

All four of the men looked like they had been living out of saddle bags too long. Their disheveled look and lack of hygiene spoke poorly of them. "By whose authority are you out here?" Karl asked.

"By God, I am the authority!" the man snapped.

Poco stood wide-eyed watching the exchange. Karl noticed that the cooks hand was inside the wagon, where Karl hoped that he kept a revolver. "You could have saved yourselves several days travel had you come and asked us the first day we spotted you."

Karl could hear others coming up from the herd. He could tell that the men he faced were becoming anxious. The man wearing the badge spit, then wiped his mouth with the back of his hand. "Get them papers out now, or by God there will be trouble!" he snarled.

"Why didn't Sheriff Wilson come with you?" Karl asked.

"He's a busy man and don't have time to chase the likes of you."

Had there been any question of whether these men were sent from Tyler, not knowing that the sheriff's name was Benson proved that they were up to no good.

Karl took a deep breath and looked the man in the eye. "In the next few seconds you are going to be dead. Your men may get a bullet in me, but it won't save you."

"You ain't even got your hand on your gun," the man blustered.

"No, but my cook behind you does, and the men behind me will get your men. So, if you want to keep breathing, you best climb on that horse and ride out of here. If we so much as suspect you boys are still following us, we will come and kill every one of you sons-of-bitches!" Karl snarled.

The color drained from the man's face and he cleared his throat. "I want you to know you're going against the law."

"Well, you tell that to *Benson*, the sheriff of Tyler."

Karl sat watching the men ride away, anger still coursing through his body. Poco looked up at his boss. "I couldn't shoot a man," he confessed as he pulled out the jug of molasses he had been reaching for.

Smiling at the cook, Karl told him, "Now, I'm glad you didn't have to."

Turning his horse, he looked at the men spread around the wagon. He felt pride in the crew. His trained soldiers couldn't have done better.

For the next couple of days, Karl had Haat range out around the herd, looking for any sign of the four men. They must have taken his threat to heart, because not a track was found.

Eleven days into the drive, they arrived at the Red River. The river was surrounded by bluffs of the same color. The rains that had given them water on the trail now caused a challenge at the river.

It was late when they reached the Red River, so the herd was bedded down on the south side. Poco had the chuck wagon upwind of the herd and was busy making supper.

Josh came and sat with Karl. "I can't swim, Karl. The river is so high, I'm not sure if I can get across."

Karl scratched his chin. "We got a bunch of rivers to cross, Josh. Didn't you think about that? All you and Tony talked about is the excitement of cowboying and driving cattle."

Josh looked at the river. "It sounded a lot easier in the dime novels."

"Well Josh, you have no choice in the matter. We got a river in front and we need you on the drive. You got a choice of riding across on the chuck wagon or clinging to the back of your horse."

He looked at the chuck wagon and the river. It seemed even scarier. "Are you sure the horse will keep me up?" Josh asked.

"It will. We can trail a rope from the horse for you to grab if you fall off. You can let the animal drag you across," Karl replied. "I would recommend you hang on to the mane of your horse damn tight so you don't have to use the rope." Karl walked back to the fire to get another cup of coffee. He had the first watch on the cattle. He didn't want to doze in the saddle.

Karl slowly rode around the herd. He sang a Finnish tune that his father had taught him. Next he sang some songs from church. It didn't matter what you sang around the longhorns. They seemed content to know who was wandering around them.

Coyotes were active this night. He could hear them yapping as they closed in on their prey. An owl hooted. There were over 1,000 cows next to him and James riding opposite him, yet the night felt lonely.

Karl started singing a song that brought Karen to mind. Not a day went by that he didn't think about her. He looked at the moon. It was just about full. "Just maybe she's looking at the moon right now."

Karl rounded the herd and slowly moved down the other side, shaking his head. Just over a week into the drive and he was already talking to himself.

Karl was relieved at 2 AM. He pulled off his boots and put his money belt under his blanket. Using his saddle as a pillow, he pulled the blanket over his shoulder. Within minutes he was sleeping.

At breakfast, the river looked no calmer. Poco got the chuck wagon closed up and ready to go.

"Don't you worry about me, Señor Karl. I sealed the wagon, so if I get washed away I can float all the way to the Mississippi."

Karl nodded, then pointed out, "Trouble is, we would get mighty hungry waiting for you to paddle back."

Poco had always set the wagon up with two horses. He said that all a proper chuck wagon needed was two. Karl noticed that he had four horses on the wagon this morning. Snapping the reins, Poco started the team into the river.

He figured that the current would wash him downstream enough to be below the large bluff across the river from him. Water splashed up from the horses' hooves. The spray soaked the chuck wagon before it was fully in the water. The water was up to the belly of the horses when the wagon bumped over the bank and entered the river.

Poco kept a constant rhythm with his reins to make sure that none of the horses decided to try and turn back. If they did, the wagon would be swamped and Poco would be swimming for his life.

Suddenly, the lead horses had to start swimming. As they continued, all the horses were swimming, waves splashing over their backs, and the wagon floated behind. Poco stood in the front of the wagon like it was a chariot. He snapped the reins across the horses and shouted encouragement.

Karl saw a log floating toward them. It hit the wagon on the back corner and knocked the tailgate open. Water splashed onto the pots located near the edge.

It was a sight to see. Poco, standing bravely, facing the raging river, bringing the team through. He barely got the team across before the next bluff. Dripping and shaking, the team stood on the far bank.

Poco waved back. "Not a problem. Bring them over."

Josh took more than a little kidding from the other men when they saw him sitting on his horse, his face white with fear. They moved the herd a little further upstream before they put them into the water. Poco's crossing was a good gauge at how far they would float down.

Haat stayed with the herd for the crossing. They set up with three men on each side and three pushing the herd for the crossing. Josh and Albert joined Karl at the back.

The herd crossed the river, spraying water, their long horns knocking together. The cattle bawled and rolled their eyes. The ones in the water couldn't turn back because they were being pushed by the ones entering.

The first riders reached the other side, dripping wet. They had their hands full moving the cattle away from the river to make room for the others to come ashore. Karl saw three cattle floating on their sides downstream. He wondered how many others he had not seen.

Josh entered the water on his horse and clung to the mane like his life depended on it. Maybe it did. At last, the herd was across. Some cows were lost, but all the men driving the herd made it. Harry had brought the horses across without any problems. They had enough wild mustang in them that crossing a river was not difficult.

Moving the herd away from the Red River, Karl was bringing up the drag when he heard a cow bellowing behind. Looking, he saw that one that had been washed beyond the second bluff. It had made it ashore and was looking for the herd. Karl was glad to see that there was one less loss.

A mile from the river, they bunched the herd to give them time to graze and rest. There was also the hope that a few more stragglers would catch up. The crew had gotten a good soaking, so Karl kept an eye on the herd while the men stripped down to dry their boots and clothing.

Karl couldn't help but chuckle at the sight of the cowboys running around barefoot in their long johns. Poco had the fire going and coffee on. With the help of Mel, the cook was butchering one of the animals that was injured during the crossing. He would be making steaks in the large, black cast iron frying pan for their supper.

After putting on dry clothes, Tony rode in to relieve his brother. "The coffee is hot and Poco put out some corn bread from last night."

Karl looked at the grasslands of Oklahoma north of them. "We got a month of driving the cattle through Choctaw, Comanche, Creek, and other tribes' territory. We'll be sleeping light for some time."

"Yes, but we have a Ho-Chunk for a brother, and with his help we will do okay," Tony said with a good measure of pride in his voice.

They were six to eight weeks from Kansas City. The monotony of the drive made it difficult for the men to stay alert. The daily routine varied little. Travel across Oklahoma was mostly on grassy plains. They saw herds of buffalo. Haat killed a good sized cow buffalo. He and Poco butchered the animal and everyone enjoyed the meat.

Haat called Karl aside. "I saw unshod pony tracks today. They watch us pass. They have buffalo meat to eat, so it is not cattle they want. It will be horses, scalps, and guns."

Karl looked at the rolling plains. A whole tribe could hide in any one of the dips. He knew they were undermanned with only 10 men. While they could handle the herd okay, if there were problems with weather, herd cutters, or Indians, they would be stretched too thin.

Karl held a meeting that night after supper. All the men gathered around the cook fire, except John and Mel, who were watching the herd. Karl began.

"We are now in the toughest part of the drive. Haat found some sign of Indians today. The weather has been dry, so there is also a chance of a sand storm. Whatever trouble it is, we need to be ready. Starting tonight, we need to double the watch on the herd. The herd will be pushed 12 hours each day."

"The herd likes to string out. They will have to be kept bunched. The extra horses will be kept close to the herd. If we are attacked by Indians, leave the herd and head for the chuck wagon. We will try and make a stand from that point. Each night we will try and stop the herd in a defendable position."

"At night we will split into two watch groups each three-hours long. Josh and Tony will join Albert and John. Mel, Harry, James and I will relieve them in three hours. Poco will keep coffee going and plenty of biscuits. Haat will scout for trouble."

Karl thought for a moment. "One more thing. Everyone will carry their saddle bags on their horses with extra ammunition and food. Carry your rifle and any spare revolvers. Keep your canteens full. If we have to make a stand, let your horses go, but keep these with you."

Karl walked to the edge of the fire. He didn't know if the extra measures would do a single bit of good if they were attacked by Indians. They would help in case of storms, and even herd cutters. Karl felt the weight of leadership on his shoulders. The war had prepared him for this, but he never liked it. He watched Tony and Haat getting their mounts ready.

Haat led his horse past Karl. "Do you want me to talk to Mel and John?"

Karl shook his head. "I'll ride down with you and let them know."

Before leaving, he called Harry over. "If there is an attack, try and split the horses and send half running toward the Indians. It might slow them a bit, deciding if they should grab them or keep attacking. Haat and I will try and help if we can.

After talking with Mel and John, Karl rode back to the fire for a last cup of coffee before turning in. Poco was making biscuits.

Seeing Karl, he pointed to some biscuits fresh out of the Dutch oven. "Help yourself, Señor Karl. Breakfast will be quick tomorrow, so I wanted these to be ready."

"Thank you, Poco."

"You are doing the right things for the safety of the men and the herd, Señor Karl. I have been on many drives. You can't prevent attacks or storms. You can only try and be prepared."

Karl accepted the hot biscuits, moved into the darkness and drank his coffee. He was worried. They could not afford to lose many of the cattle. There would not be enough from the sale to pay off the note. Staring into the dark, he strained his ears for any sound. Odds were that any attack would come in the early morning. Karl finally turned in and slept fitfully until woken for his watch.

The sun was hot in the Oklahoma sky as they drove the herd. It had been three days since the last Indian sign had been found by Haat. Karl made it a habit to range around the herd, watching for trouble.

James was doing his share to drive the cattle and had apparently run out of whiskey. Karl hadn't seen any bottles lately.

Karl was riding flank when Tony came and relieved him. The chuck wagon was staying close to the herd, so he rode up and got two biscuits and some cold meat from Poco. Before starting again, the Mexican checked his team and wagon.

Josh and John were riding drag. The wind was blowing east and keeping the dust off them. James was on the left flank with Mel. Harry had the horses close to the right flank of the herd, near Tony and Albert. Haat was ranging in front of them. The grass was an unbroken expanse of brown, rolling prairie. Finishing his meal, Karl watched Poco start the chuck wagon team. He was thinking about riding up with Haat for a bit when there was a shout from the herd.

"Indians!" Tony was shouting. "Indians!"

About two dozen Comanches swept down the left flank of the herd. Karl pulled his rifle and fired two shots into the air. Poco looked back and jumped from the wagon to unhitch the team. Josh and John were riding hard toward Karl. Harry did his best to send some of the horses running at the Comanches before heading for the wagon. Haat was riding toward the chuck wagon at a full gallop.

Tony and Albert pulled up at the chuck wagon and started to return fire at the attacking warriors.

Karl looked on in disbelief as he saw James draw his revolver and start trying to stampede the cattle, firing into the air and shouting. Mel was trying to get across the herd and make for the chuck wagon.

The sun glistened off the naked, bronzed bodies of the Comanche warriors. Karl could see the streaks of war paint on them and their horses. Many were carrying single-shot rifles.

Karl watched helplessly as the cattle surrounded Mel, knocking his horse down. He could hear Mel's cries as the cattle ran over him. With the Comanches closing in on them, Karl realized that the startled herd was heading toward the chuck wagon.

James was spurring his horse toward Karl, with the Comanches close on his heels. His horse faltered when hit by a Comanche bullet. James went over the horse's head as it collapsed under him. Rolling with the fall, he jumped to his feet. He stood with his legs spread and began emptying his spare revolver at the oncoming warriors. Karl heard Josh cry out when the Comanches overran James.

Karl saw James' last act of defiance as he grabbed a warrior by the hair and loin cloth. Raising the warrior over his head, James threw him as the charging Comanches riddled his body with bullets and arrows.

Poco leaped onto the back of the unhitched team and got them out of the way before the herd surrounded the chuck wagon. Fortunately, Albert's and Tony's horses stood ground reined. They leapt onto the horses and followed Poco.

It became a desperate race for a defendable position. Karl waited until those who were left caught up to him, taking careful shots with his rifle at the charging Comanches.

Then, as a group, they headed across the Oklahoma prairie. Karl could see the tops of some trees in a swale ahead of them and directed the group to ride for them. The war cries of the Comanches sent chills up their spines as the Indians gained ground on them.

Galloping over the rise before the swale, Karl couldn't believe his eyes. In front of them was a stone cabin. The roof was mostly caved in and the door was gone, but the walls looked solid.

"Ride for the cabin!" Karl yelled.

He felt something tug his sleeve and heard gun fire coming from the cabin at them. They scattered but continued toward the safety of the stone walls. There was another shot. Based on the rate of fire, someone was using a muzzle loader. They leaped to the ground in front of the cabin. Grabbing their saddle bags and slapping the horses, they charged through the open door, Tony and Albert leading the way.

A wide-eyed girl sat in a corner holding a Kentucky long rifle. She was trying to reload it. Everyone spread out to find a position that they could defend and started returning fire at the Comanches.

The repeater rifles were probably all that saved them. They were able to put up a field of fire from the stone cabin that broke the attack. Several warriors were knocked from their horses with the first two volleys.

The stone cabin had been designed to be defended from attacks coming from any direction. There were openings on all sides to shoot from. The Comanches circled the building a couple of times before they disappeared back over the rise, in the direction of the herd.

Suddenly, everything was quiet. Karl became aware of the girl with the long rifle. She had stringy blond hair and a sunburned face. Her dress was torn and dirty. She was barefoot, with cuts and scratches on her legs.

Tony moved over to the girl. "Are you okay? I mean, were you hurt during the attack?"

She looked around the room at them. "You aren't them. . . You brought the Indians down on me."

"We didn't have a choice. We were attacked. I don't know who 'them' are, but my name is Tony August."

"I'm Ruth Collins. They killed my . . . my family." She began to cry long, racking sobs.

Karl realized that they were looking at a girl who had just come to the end of a terrible ordeal. Somehow her family had been killed, leaving her alone on the prairie. She was thin and hollow-eyed.

Karl looked around the room. Tony, Josh, John, Albert, Poco, and Harry had made it to the building. Haat was missing and possibly dead. He knew that James and Mel were dead. Josh stared unblinking out an opening, clutching his Sharps rifle. His face showed the pain that he was feeling for his brother as he fought back the tears.

John, Poco and Harry had taken up positions on the other three walls. Karl moved to the doorway near Albert and looked out at the bodies of the Comanches killed or wounded during the attack. He watched as one dragged himself out of sight, over the rise.

Karl had no idea if they would be attacked again. He knew that there was ammunition and food for a short duration. He had noticed a shallow well dug into one corner of the building. It held adequate water. Poco carried a pack on his back filled with extra food and some ammunition.

Tony sat with the girl, talking softly. She had quit crying. Karl had seen the same type of reactions during the war. Men would hold their emotions in during a battle. When it was over and the immediate danger of being killed was gone, they thought of the friends who had been lost and they would break down.

The sun was low in the sky. They just built a small fire to prepare a meal when Karl heard movement outside. He grabbed up the Henry rifle and moved to the doorway.

"It's me, Haat. Don't shoot."

Haat stumbled into the cabin. He had a bruise on the side of his head and a deep gash across his back, above the shoulder blades. His buckskin shirt was wet with blood down the back.

"Come over here Haat," Harry said. "I got some stuff in my saddlebags to fix you up."

Haat removed his shirt and sat next to the fire. John handed him a cup of coffee and Haat took a sip.

"The fight make you change your mind about coffee?" Tony inquired.

Haat tried to smile. "It's hot. The awful taste will make me forget about the pain."

"You be quiet now, Haat, and quit moving. I'll get you cleaned and fixed up." Harry dipped a cloth into a pot of hot water next to the fire and began washing the wound.

Karl sat alone in front of the stone cabin. Looking at the stars, he fought the feelings of being overwhelmed. His thoughts went to his father. How had Oli managed during the long winter alone in the Black Hills? He'd had a dead man as his only companion and wolves at the door. There had been the constant threat of being found by Indians.

His father, Oli, had taken refuge from the wolves in a cabin. In it, he'd found the body of Don Sikes. Unable to bury him in the frozen ground, he'd placed the body in a corner until spring.

Closing his eyes, he could see his father's blond hair and blue eyes. He'd had a quick smile when telling stories about the family back in Finland, and a sober look when giving instructions on survival in the wilderness.

When Karl was young, he would awake to the sounds of his mother and father talking softly over cups of coffee. He would lay quiet, not wanting to disturb them during their private time.

The moon was almost full in the eastern sky. Once again, he thought of Karen. He remembered the way that she tossed her hair. He could see them together, enjoying morning coffee. Haat stepped out of the cabin, breaking his train of thought.

"We need to look for horses in the morning," Haat said as he sat favoring the wound on his back.

"If the Comanches don't come back in the morning, we'll start looking," Karl said.

The two men sat looking into the darkness and listening to the night. Haat began to talk in low tones so that the others could not hear.

"James scattered herd. He drove them over Mel and at the chuck wagon. I do not think he wanted to hurt anyone. He saw a chance to leave you without many cattle." Haat continued. "It was James who opened the brush fence. I found his tracks next to where the brush was dragged."

Sighing, Karl agreed. "I know that, Haat. I believe he was sent with us to make sure a herd was never delivered. He was following his father's orders." Looking in the direction of the fire, he could see Josh sitting with his head hanging. "I don't think Josh knew what his brother was doing."

Haat sat quietly for a moment. "James' stand against the Comanche gave us time. Standing there shooting, he slowed them while we got away."

Karl nodded. "It is probably the best way to remember him. That memory will help Josh get through the loss."

He stopped by the fire before turning in and took the note on hotel stationary from the money belt. He watched as the fire turned the note to ash. Nothing would be gained by discrediting the dead. Karl saw that Tony was sleeping near the girl. Josh was sleeping alone to the side. He spread his blanket next to him.

Karl awoke to the smell of side meat frying over the fire. Poco was unbelievable. Karl wondered how much stuff he had in the back pack.

He suddenly realized that he had overslept. He had gotten very little rest the past week. He gave himself a mental scolding for letting his guard down, but admitted that he felt a lot better.

Haat was looking out the door. "The bodies are gone. I think the Comanches have left."

Accepting a cup of coffee from Poco, Karl joined Haat at the doorway.

"I looked around," Haat said. "I think they were after the horses. They chased us in the spirit of the raid. Our guns were more than their strong medicine. They settled for our horses. The horses will give them wealth and power in the tribe."

"Where are Albert and Harry?" Karl asked.

149

"They are looking for horses nearby. I warned them to move carefully."

Josh and John were on watch in front of the cabin. Tony was watching Poco get breakfast ready while keeping an eye on Ruth.

Ruth was just finishing up washing near the shallow well. Some effort had been made to fix her dress and remove some of the dust. Haat carried an extra pair of moccasins in his saddlebags. He had modified them enough to fit Ruth.

The worst cut on her leg had a poultice and bandage. She had combed her hair out. Karl was surprised to see how pretty she was. It wasn't lost on Tony, either.

Harry came into the stone cabin and sat down near the fire. Taking a cold biscuit, he dipped it into the meat grease and took a large bite. Chewing the biscuit, he enjoyed the mouthful. He swallowed and turned to Karl.

"We found the wagon team down near the trees. They were tangled in the brush. I figure the Comanches didn't want to bother with them. Also found your buckskin and saddle. It is tied out front."

"Thank you, Harry. After breakfast you can join me and Haat. We will be looking over the damage on the other side of the rise."

Poco piped up, "I will go also, Señor Karl. I will bring the chuck wagon back here and fix it."

John and Albert were assigned to keep watch, while Tony and Josh cleaned up the stone cabin and made what remained of the roof more stable. Ruth was still very tired from lack of food and needed to rest.

Karl noticed that Haat had an unshod pony with his saddle on it. Harry and Poco each climbed onto the team horses while Karl swung onto the buckskin.

Karl kidded Haat, "Nice pony you got there."

Haat squinted and smiled at Karl. "When I heard your shots yesterday, I saw the Comanches coming in. I headed for the chuck wagon as we planned. James stampeded the herd and it got between me and the wagon."

"Five warriors came after me for a quick scalp. I rode west to top of the next rise and stopped to face them. A bullet hit my horse, barely missing my leg. I threw myself away from the horse as it went down and then used it as cover."

"I was able to shoot two of the Comanches before they got to me. One jumped his horse over my dead horse and a hoof clipped my head. It knocked me out of the way of an arrow that may have hit me. The three went by me and turned to finish me off."

"I used my last shot at the one with the bow. The other two had an empty rifle and a spear. The one with the spear threw it as he rode by, cutting my back. Then they must have gone after the horses. The two rode away, forgetting me."

"It took me some time to catch and saddle this unshod pony."

Riding over the rise, Karl's heart sank. Secretly, he had hoped to see several of the cattle bunched and waiting. Instead, all that remained was an overturned chuck wagon and a horse standing on three legs with its head hanging. There were two dozen longhorns dead and bloated across the valley.

Poco and Harry rode down to survey the chuck wagon. Karl and Haat rode over to check on the horse. It was Mel's horse. The saddle was slung around its belly, and it was bruised and bloodied from its ordeal with the longhorns.

"You check the horse over, Haat, and I'll go look for Mel and James."

Karl turned the buckskin toward something a hundred yards from the horse. It was Mel's crumpled body. Karl's stomach turned when he saw what was left. He had seen worse during the war when a cannon ball exploded near a line of men. But he never got used to seeing a body that resembled chopped meat more than a man.

The buzzing of the flies was loud. They had found the body and were busy feeding and laying eggs. He wished that he had something to cover Mel with. He continued south through the valley and came upon James. He had been scalped and mutilated. Josh couldn't see his brother like this.

Karl rode back to the chuck wagon. Poco and Harry had it back on its wheels. They were busy sorting and putting any good items back into the wagon.

Karl heard a shot. He knew that Haat had to put down the injured horse. He saw Haat leading his horse and carrying Mel's saddle. Mel's saddlebags were slung over Haat's horse.

"It had a broken leg. Damn shame, it was a good-looking horse." Haat tossed the saddle into the front of the chuck wagon.

"Why don't you scout around, Haat, and see if you can find any sign of cattle or horses? I'll go pick up Mel and James." Karl had no desire to go back to the bodies, but could not justify sending someone else.

Karl watched Haat ride away in the direction in which the herd had gone. Poco and Harry had the chuck wagon hitched up and ready to drive back to the stone cabin.

Poco walked up to Karl. "It could have been worse. We lost some food and one spoke on a wheel is broken. Other than that, the cattle didn't do too much damage, Señor Karl. The Comanches must have been busy going after the horses and didn't have time to ransack the wagon."

"Thanks, Poco. See if you can find me a couple of ground tarps to wrap the bodies in."

Harry heard Karl's request and came around the wagon with two tarps. "I'll help you, Mista Karl. I seen worse than those below before. It'll take more than one man to put things together in the tarps."

"Thanks, Harry. Also, grab some rope to tie the tarps."

The chuck wagon was sitting in front of the stone cabin as Karl and Harry came down the rise leading the buckskin with two bodies draped over it. The sun was hot on their backs. Smoke was rising from the open section of the roof and Karl could smell beans with molasses cooking. He also got a whiff of biscuits baking.

Karl saw John holding a shovel near two open graves off to the side of the stone cabin. He noticed that there were some older graves nearby. John walked toward them.

"Which one is Mel? I want to get him into the ground before more flies get to him. You can leave James out for the buzzards to pick at as far as I am concerned."

Karl pointed to Mel's body. "I know how you feel John, but remember Josh. What James did was not Josh's fault, and he is feeling bad about losing a brother."

"I know, Karl, but I am mad clear through. Don't worry, I dug both graves good and deep."

Haat had not gotten back when they held the funerals. In the heat the bodies would turn quickly and it was an odor no one should have to experience before supper. Josh stood quietly staring at the mound of dirt over James as Albert struggled to say some meaningful words over the two men. John said a few things about his departed friend and then led them in a hymn.

Karl was glad that the two men were buried. He could now start looking to the future. They would first have to see how many cattle they could find. Harry had found two more horses a ways down the swale. One had John's saddle. That made four riding horses and two for the chuck wagon.

Poco had repaired the wheel spoke and had the wagon back in shape and ready to go. He had moved the cook fire out of the stone cabin. They didn't need the added heat inside.

Tony carved James' and Mel's names on two pieces of board and set them at the head of the graves. Josh and Ruth were with him. Karl noticed that Josh stayed behind at the graves after Tony and Ruth came back to the fire. He saw Josh kneel and pray over his brother. The healing had begun.

Haat came back just before dark with good news.

"About a mile north I found nine horses feeding near a small pond. One has Tony's saddle on it. I saw several bunches of cattle grazing between the horses and here." Haat took a good portion of beans and biscuits and sat down.

"That is good news indeed. Were you able to estimate the number of cattle?" Karl asked.

"Nowhere near what we had in the herd, Karl. We should find more as we go on. They like the grass in this valley."

Haat wiped the last of his beans with the remainder of a biscuit and ate it. "I would like to take Harry and go for the horses tonight. We will drive them back in the morning so they can be used to start rounding up cattle."

"See any sign of Comanches?" Karl asked.

"None at all," Haat replied. "They wanted horses. They are headed back to their teepees to sing songs of their success.

CHAPTER 10

The sun blazed down on the brittle, brown grass of the prairie. Dust devils swirled by the men as they worked rounding up the cattle. An occasional wolf skulked along the knolls, watching the progress of the men and looking for any opportunity for a meal. The men would shoot any injured animals and take some of the meat. The wolf would howl, bringing others to feast on the remains.

Karl looked into wide, blue sky. He could see a hawk floating on the wind currents. Its lonesome cries matched how Karl felt.

They had been rounding cattle up for five days, moving north as they collected them. So far, they had about 550 head. They had found one more horse and that made of total of 16, including the unshod pony.

The last day they had found two longhorns, one being the broken-horned steer. Water was becoming scarcer, and the heat was not doing the cattle any good. They had to move on.

They had left the safety of the stone cabin behind and were trying to leave the memories of the attack with it. Ruth slept in the front of the chuck wagon. With the bedrolls out at night, there was plenty of room. They had to go back to having two men watch the herd at night.

Karl and Tony sat around the fire. Albert and John were watching the herd while Harry and Josh had turned in. They would stand the next watch. Poco was snoring under the chuck wagon. Haat slept away from the rest, so he could hear any danger.

"Karl, I like Ruth," Tony confided.

"I noticed that, Tony."

"I want to marry her when this is over."

It didn't surprise Karl. "You'll be 17 when this is over. You'll be a man."

"She talked to me about what happened." Tony paused as Karl waited.

"Her father had a farm about three days' walk from the stone cabin. She and her mother were doing the wash. Her brother and father were working in the field. Her mother sent her to get more water from the stream. She had stopped to watch some otter playing when she heard shots."

"Ruth looked over the bank of the stream and saw her father and brother lying on the ground. Five horsemen were riding toward their cabin. Ruth said that she froze watching the attack. Her mother had run into the house and grabbed the long rifle. Before she could shoot, the horsemen rode her down."

"They went into the cabin, looking for anything of value. They had little for them to steal. Ruth heard them swearing when they came out of the cabin. One of the men wore a Confederate coat and rode a large, black horse. He shot her mother."

Tony stopped for a moment. Karl saw that his eyes were blazing and his jaw was tight. Clearing his throat, Tony continued.

"After they rode away to the north, Ruth ran to her mother. She was dead. She got to her brother and father. Her father was still alive, but unconscious. She dragged her father back to the cabin and put him in the bed and tried to fix his wounds. He had two bullet holes in his back and one in his stomach. Her brother had been shot in the back and the head. He was only 13 years-old. Ruth buried her mother and brother that day. Two days later, she buried her father."

Tony wiped his nose. "Ruth was afraid that the men might come back, so she took the long rifle and ran south from the farm. She lost her shoes and pack of food crossing a river. She managed to hang onto the rifle and powder horn. She was resting in the stone cabin when she heard shots. She saw us coming over the rise and thought we might be more men like the ones that shot her family."

Karl sat, absorbing what Tony had told him. He had known teams of men who were tasked to raid the enemy. Both sides had them. They were given broad discretion in what they did. Some were unnecessarily cruel. After the war, some of these men continued. They liked intimidating people and looking for easy money.

The wind had begun to blow and the smell of rain was in the air. The rain they could use. It was the end of August. The summer had been dry on the prairie. Many of the smaller streams were dry. This meant that they would have to drive the cattle farther, keeping to larger tributaries. It would take more time, which they did not have.

They woke to a cooling rain. The wind had blown the clouds in. Poco had a fly tarp up to keep them dry during breakfast. The cattle were up and busy grazing on the wet brown grass. Karl finished his breakfast and watched the others kidding and joking. The freshness of the rain had brought renewed spirit.

Karl called the group together. Even the men watching the herd came in. They had a good view of the cattle from the campsite.

"I have made a decision on our destination," Karl began. "We drive the herd to Kansas City. Once there, the 200 head of Hal Wooden will be sold and the money sent to him. We will then take the remaining cattle and drive them to Fort Dakota. There, I hope we can get $30 a head. Finish up your coffee and we will get the herd moving."

The rain had lasted two days. Karl was impressed over how fast the prairie started to green up. They took advantage of the better grass and water, pushing the herd from dawn to dusk each day. Karl estimated that it would take three more weeks to make Kansas City.

Karl awoke before daylight and helped Poco with the morning cook fire. The rain was now only a memory. There were flowers on the prairie. Paintbrush, buttercups, and daisies could be seen. Bees, birds, and butterflies were everywhere.

The cattle were handling well, and the crew's spirits remained good. Ruth rode with Poco and was a great help with meals. She and Tony spend a lot of time talking. Karl noticed the Josh seemed alone without his best friend and the loss of his brother. He mentioned this to Albert and the two of them decided to try and spend more time with him.

While all appeared well, Karl was worried. They were now working with an impossibly thin margin. If they lost any more cattle, the note could not be satisfied. He thought about all the work and planning that had been done. It would be a shame if it had been for nothing.

Two longhorns had dropped out due to leg problems in the past week. One had severe swelling on a rear leg joint. The other had hurt its leg in a prairie dog hole. Poco butchered the second one. The first was just left behind to heal and fend for itself.

Two weeks out of Kansas City, Karl counted the cattle. He was surprised to find that additional cattle were missing. The only explanation was that some had wandered off during the night, or were stolen by Indians. They could have been cutting the herd at night. It was not unusual for the herd to spread out looking for grass. They needed them to graze to maintain weight.

They were camped in a broad valley with a wide, shallow stream. Oak trees lined the creek. The cattle had spent the night grazing or sleeping. Their coats were sleek and they were in good shape.

Karl knew that he had encouraged letting the cattle spread out to graze, hoping to get the maximum price at the time of sale. He now knew that the strategy was not working. Tony was tightening the cinch on a grulla. Karl led his buckskin over to him.

"We have been losing cattle at night."

"You know, Karl, I was wondering myself. I was hoping it was my imagination, but I was going to talk to you about that."

"I have had Haat ranging out, looking for water and grazing," Karl said. "We need to bring him back in. We need to push the herd hard and get them to Kansas City."

Three days out of Kansas City, they were bringing the cattle over a rise when they saw six horsemen coming toward them. Poco stopped the chuck wagon short of the men, staying just east of the herd. Karl was on the left flank. He watched as Haat, Tony, John, and Harry spread out. Albert stayed at the drag and Josh moved up to the chuck wagon.

Karl and Tony rode ahead to meet the men. They were carrying their Colts, but not their rifles. Being short of extra horses, Karl didn't want them carrying extra weight. The men stopped four abreast, with two remaining to the back.

"We have the right of way. I must ask you to let our cattle pass," Karl said with a hint of anger in his voice.

The two riders from the back came forward to the left of the others. One was a big man wearing a worn Confederate uniform and riding a trail-weary black. The other five men had the same shoddy look about them. All wore parts of Confederate uniforms. They all had clean rifles balanced across their saddles. A jolt went through the brothers, remembering Ruth's story of the attack on the farm.

The big man spit his chaw on the ground. His eyes never left Karl. "That, we can do. But first, there is a small fee that must be paid for passing. Right now, your cattle are trampling my grazing land. You can pay with cash money or cows."

"I doubt that is the case," Karl growled. "I see no evidence of cattle on this land. In fact, I don't even believe you are from this area. It looks like your boys have been riding hard."

Knowing these men were ruthless, Karl's mind was racing. Even if given money, they would probably stampede the herd and picked off as many men and horses at they could before riding away. There was a good chance he and Tony would be shot first.

The riders with the big man began to look about nervously. What Karl and Tony couldn't see was that Haat, John, and Harry had outflanked the group. They sat on their horses with guns drawn. In an attempt to intimidate Karl and Tony, the big man snarled, "You don't want to turn this into a shooting war. My boys will drill you before you can clear leather."

From behind Tony and Karl, Haat replied, "It won't matter to you, because you are the first one I will shoot."

Realizing they had been outmaneuvered by what should have been easy pickings, the big man warned, "You win this round cowboy, but I suggest you sleep light from now on." He pulled his horse over to leave.

The shot that came from the direction of the chuck wagon was completely unexpected. Karl saw part of the big man's head blown away, taking his hat with it. The rest of the big man's men, caught off guard, brought their rifles up and fired too quickly. Their shots went just wide of their targets, one clipping the back of Tony's saddle.

Karl and Tony drew their revolvers. Almost as one they squeezed off shots at the two men nearest them. Karl scored a hit dead center, while Tony's shot went through the arm of the other man, causing his rifle to fall on the ground. They fought to control their horses while they continued firing.

Karl heard shots all around him. A bullet tugged his sleeve. He saw the man whom Tony had wounded reaching for his revolver, using a cross draw. Karl leveled his Army Colt on the man and put a bullet just to the right of his middle shirt button.

Suddenly, all was quiet. The six men lay dead or dying on the prairie grass. Karl watched as Ruth walked up to the big man and smashed his dead face into a pulp with the butt of the long rifle.

"You killed my family!" Ruth screamed. "For what? We had nothing worth killing for!"

Tony swung down from his horse and took Ruth in his arms. She dropped the long rifle as Tony led her back to the chuck wagon.

Karl suddenly realized that it had been Ruth who had shot the big man. She had recognized him as the one who had attacked her family. Her actions had given them the advantage over the cold-blooded bunch.

Five of the men were dead. The sixth was gut shot. Karl had seen many men shot the same way while in the army. After a few pain-filled days, they always died. He wished this suffering on no one.

Karl was relieved to find out that his crew had incurred only minor wounds. John had been burned on the shoulder, and Poco was grazed on the cheek. He remembered feeling the tug on his sleeve and found a neat hole just above the cuff. Other than that, the rest of the crew came out of the fray unscathed.

The five men were buried in shallow graves. The gut shot man was put into the chuck wagon. Haat had applied a poultice and bandage to the wound

After saying a few words over the graves, they moved the herd out. It was then that Karl noticed five longhorns that were unable to continue, due to bullet wounds. Harry and Poco remained behind. Karl heard the shots as they put the wounded animals out of their misery.

To nobody in particular he said, "And we carry one of the men that helped cause our losses while we wait for him to die."

As it turned out, the wounded man, Hap Tenny, had just joined the other five two days before. He was just looking for someone to ride with to Kansas City. The big man's name was Clem Davis. He'd convinced Hap to join them. The plan was to grab a few cattle to sell and buy whiskey and women.

CHAPTER 11

Kansas City was wild and exciting. While it was dusty and had the smell of cattle pens, the saloons were brightly lit. The night air was filled with piano music and the shrill laughter of ladies. Cowboys fresh off the trail whooped it up, spending hard-earned wages on whiskey, women, or losing it to crooked gamblers.

Karl kept the cattle a couple miles west of the town. Most of the grass had been grazed off. He could see other herds, larger than theirs, waiting to be sold.

Tony and Poco escorted Ruth and stopped at the mercantile. A potbellied man with a crisp white shirt stood behind the counter. A short, plump woman with her hair in a tight bun was arranging canned goods on a shelf. They both turned and smiled as the three entered.

"What can we do for you?" the man said.

He suddenly stared at Ruth, having just noticed the conditions of her clothes. "My goodness. What happened to you?"

Being protective, Tony answered for her, "Her family was killed on the prairie and she narrowly escaped. We need some clothes for Ruth here and a place for her to stay."

The portly lady stepped forward quickly. "Edward, take some clothes to the spare room. Heat some water for a bath. I'll help the young lady select some shoes. Right now, Edward!"

Edward hurried to the back at his wife's direction. He carried two dresses and other necessities with him.

"Come with me, dear. My name is Clara. You can stay with us while you are in town."

Clara motioned to Tony and Poco. "You gents look around for what you need. Edward will be right back to settle up."

Tony and Poco stood with mouths open and looked around the store.

"I wonder if we can get some credit until we sell some cows," Poco said.

Karl borrowed a buckboard from the livery to bring the wounded Hap Tenny into town. After dropping him off at the doctor's, Karl went to see the sheriff. The husky sheriff was sitting on the porch in front of the jail. He had a smoke-stained moustache and clenched a short pipe in his teeth. Leather suspenders held up his wool britches. Dusty boots with worn heels covered his feet and a tarnished star was pinned to his faded shirt.

"I'm Sheriff Ralston. Saw you bring the man in to Doc's. Who is he and what happened?"

Karl quickly filled the sheriff in on what happened out on the prairie. The sheriff was familiar with the name Clem Davis. He had heard that the man was headed his way and was happy to hear that he had been dealt with.

"You know, young man, we don't need more trouble in this town. We got all the cowboys shaking out the kinks. Mostly good men, but with a belly full of cheap whiskey and an agitator like Clem Davis, some would likely have gotten shot."

The sheriff took a long draw on his pipe. Blowing the smoke out through his nose, he continued. "Townspeople expect me to do something about the shootings. When two grown men draw down on each other, the fight is considered fair. It doesn't matter if the likes of Clem Davis are experienced killers. There is just nothing I can do. We go through the dead cowboy's pockets and if there is enough money left, we use it to bury him. If not, the town picks up the cost."

Karl motioned toward the doctor's. "If Tenny there should happen to live, what happens to him?"

"Well, I am sure you don't plan to stick around. It will be hard to have a trial without witnesses. If you leave us his horse, I will put him up on it and send him out of town. Maybe he will think about the company he keeps in the future."

Karl watched the sheriff tap his pipe on the heel of his boot, knocking the ash out. "It would be my guess, sheriff, that Mr. Tenny won't live to ride out of town. We will bring his horse and saddle to you. You can sell them to pay the doc and bury him decent."

He started away, then turned back to the sheriff. "Can you recommend any buyers who would be interested in a couple hundred cows?"

The sheriff gave Karl a couple names of cattle buyers who could be trusted.

He arrived back at the herd just in time for supper. After a meal of beef, beans, biscuits, and canned peaches, Tony joined him with coffee.

Tony leaned against the chuck wagon wheel. "Ruth is staying with the family that owns the mercantile. They gave us some credit until we sell cattle," he said.

"That's good, Tony. Ruth will be much better off there. Maybe she can get a job at the mercantile."

"I plan to marry her before we leave, Karl. I want her to come with us."

Karl looked at the firmly set jaw of his younger brother. "Mother and Jenny won't be very happy missing the wedding."

"Don't worry, Karl. We can get married all over again once we get back to Elkader."

Karl set his coffee cup down on a nearby rock. He was not surprised that Tony wanted to get married in Kansas City. It would not be proper to have Ruth travel with them unless she and Tony were married. To find her and save her on the prairie before coming into town was considered a good thing. To leave town unmarried was frowned upon in some quarters.

Karl had their father's ledger out in his lap. While his father had kept clear lists with good notes, Karl had scribbled numbers of cattle and a couple of supply lists into the ledger. He now wrote that they had 286 cattle left after cutting Hal Wooden's share out.

Looking up at his brother, Karl said, "They are paying $17 a head right now. We arrived with too many other herds."

"That price should make Mr. Wooden happy, Karl. We have to sell a few more to cover mercantile charges and other expenses for the drive up to Fort Dakota."

"I agree. I figure if we sell 40 head, we should be okay," Karl said, making a few notes inside the ledger.

"John wants his pay. He plans to head south again with some other drovers."

Karl digested the new bit of information. "It is his right to go. He just signed on to come as far as Kansas City." Shaking his head, Karl continued. "We'll have to sell a few more cows to cover that."

Karl sat alone after Tony went to his blankets. He realized that the cattle drive had become an undertaking that would not solve anything. They had lost too many cattle to satisfy the note. They would end up with a few dollars for their mother. She would have to move. The home that they had known would be gone.

Albert and Jenny would be fine. He would be at the mill, and he would have an adventure to remember.

Maybe he and Tony could go back to Texas and put together another herd. He was sure Haat, Harry, and Poco would sign up. Next time it would be for shares.

Karl rolled into his blankets, feeling the most peace he had felt since the beginning of the trip. Once you accept the future, the solutions are much simpler. He suddenly sat up. . .

Did Tony say he was getting married?

CHAPTER 12

The wedding was small. They were joined at the small white church by Edward and Clara Wilson. Karl stood up with Tony. The Wilsons had a daughter, Sonia, who stood up with Ruth. Sheriff Ralston and his wife sat with Karl's crew.

The sheriff was a surprise. Not only did he come up with a couple of volunteers to watch the herd, he supplied chickens for a wedding picnic. The Wilsons contributed corn on the cob from their garden and Poco made a cake.

The preacher was a stocky, red-faced man with a firm, square jaw. He looked every bit the part of a hellfire and brimstone preacher. On this day he kept the ceremony about Tony and Ruth.

John had not headed back for Texas yet and sang a couple of songs. He had a fine baritone voice. The preacher did try to compete with John during the closing hymn.

The picnic was held in a grove of willows next to a babbling brook. Karl watched as everyone enjoyed the fried chicken, corn on the cob, biscuits with honey, all washed down with a drink made with raspberries, sugar, and water. There were even a couple of kids running through the willows and splashing in the brook.

Karl wondered for a moment . . . would Karen be waiting for him? Would there be a wedding in their future and, eventually, children to play beside Turkey River?

His attention was brought back to the picnic as he heard Albert and Josh coaxing Tony to give Ruth a wedding kiss. Karl was glad to see Josh joining in.

It all culminated when Poco, proud as he could be, brought out the cake. It was a two-layer cake with white frosting. He had mixed a bit of berry juice into a little of the frosting and wrote 'Tony and Ruth' on the top.

A pot of coffee was brewed, and everyone sat around eating wedding cake and drinking the raspberry drink or coffee. Haat winked at Karl and clinked his cup of raspberry drink against Karl's cup of coffee.

"We got a new sister . . . my brother," Haat said.

Three days later, Hal Wooden's cows had been sold and arrangements were made to send the money. Karl sold 45 additional cows to pay off John and finance the rest of the drive. He also sold five of the horses from Clem Davis' gang. They were in poor condition, but every dollar helped.

The Wilsons let Tony and Ruth use a cabin next to the brook so that they could have some time to themselves.

The next morning was sunny, with a comfortable breeze from the west. Sheriff Ralston walked into camp leading a horse. Karl was just finishing shaving. He rinsed his face and dumped the water from the basin.

"I brung you Tenny's horse," the sheriff said. "He died last night. The stomach wound went sour on him."

"Won't you need to sell it to bury him?" Karl asked.

"His saddle and guns paid the Doc and undertaker. You did your share bringing him in, so the horse is yours."

Karl handed the lead rope to Harry so that he could bring the horse with the others. Turning back to the sheriff, he pointed to the coffee pot.

"Join me for a hot cup of coffee, sheriff. We won't be leaving for a couple more hours."

The sheriff accepted the cup of coffee and sat on a log next to the fire. "I figured you would be leaving soon. I saw Tony and Ruth saying their goodbyes to the Wilsons. The glow on their faces makes a body feel good all over."

Karl smiled and nodded, yet he wondered about the rest of the trip. Would they run into additional problems before Fort Dakota? Driving cattle and sleeping in the open could put a strain on folks. He hoped that their newlywed frame of mind could withstand the hardships.

The cattle seemed to be happy to get back on the trail. Karl chuckled, "You old cows figured you dodged the butcher?"

The broken horn steer took his place in the lead. They were driving 241 longhorns and had a total of 15 horses. Karl and Josh rode drag, Albert and Tony were on the right flank, Harry and Haat were on the left flank and had the extra horses.

Poco and Ruth rode a little ahead of the herd in the chuck wagon. Poco had been singing a lot of Spanish songs lately. He had told Karl that the songs were good for making babies. Karl told him to save the baby songs until they finished the drive. Tony blushed brightly when Karl told him about Poco's singing.

They had about four weeks on the trail ahead of them. It was near mid-September and Karl noticed the change in the weather. Nights were getting cooler. Leaves weren't changing yet, but they would be in full color by the time they arrived at the fort.

Every night when they made camp, Ruth would help Poco get the meal ready. Haat and Karl would ride out ahead and around the herd, looking for any signs of trouble. Occasionally, they would see small groups of buffalo grazing. Haat brought down a nice whitetail buck with his bow, giving them some fresh meat.

Ruth asked Haat for the hide. She wanted to make a deerskin coat in preparation for winter. Karl and Tony looked at each other and laughed. Their father had taught them the value of a good deerskin coat. It had offered warmth, as well as needed leather, during his adventure.

Karl was still hoping to get $30 a head for the longhorns at the fort. They would have a few extra horses to sell. He would end up with $7000, give or take a little. They would need about $700 to pay off the crew. He and Tony would keep some to live on until they got back to Elkader. He hoped to have close to $6000 for his mother. It wouldn't be enough to pay off the note, but it would be enough to get a small place and some to live on.

Karl had completely accepted losing his boyhood home. His father had left the farm in Finland in 1837 and done just fine. A man who was willing to work and help others could make out okay. He couldn't understand the thinking of the Wolfe brothers. They had plenty, but it never seemed like enough.

He didn't envy Josh having to bring the news of James' death to their father, Tate Wolfe. No doubt Tate would blame them for his son's death. He would relish taking over the property and demolishing all of the buildings.

While the Wolfe brothers were some of the richest men in town, Karl believed that his father, Oli, had been a bigger man in town. There had always been talk of him showing up with old Spanish coins and rumors of where he had gotten the gold. He would not tell anyone the source. He often talked about the perils of his adventure in the West. But he had always kept the location vague.

Karl realized that the gold had helped his father and mother get their start. But it was his father's willingness to help others that had made him a success and gained him the respect of the other town folks.

They were two weeks out of Fort Dakota. Tony came in from the herd and poured himself a cup of strong, hot coffee. Ruth walked by and gave him a kiss on the cheek. She giggled when Tony whispered something to her. Then she continued down to the stream to get some water for Poco.

Tony walked over to Karl. "We lost three head this week, plus the one taken down by wolves last week. I don't know how we can stop them from wandering at night, Karl."

"Doesn't make sense, Tony. Haat wanted to track the lost cows, but we just don't have the time to stop."

"We need to be back in Elkader before the note is due. Even without the money to pay it off, I don't want our mother to have to face the Wolfe brothers alone."

Tony and Karl sat, with the herd below them in the valley. Josh and Albert were watching the cattle. Haat had ridden ahead to check out the trail. Harry was rubbing down the horses and picketing them on good grass. Poco and Ruth were cleaning up after supper while Poco sang Spanish songs.

Karl smiled at Tony and pointed to Poco. Tony pulled down his hat and continued to sip his coffee. Karl knew that he was blushing underneath the hat.

Suddenly, Tony looked up at Karl. "Would it be okay if I read some of father's ledger? Between his endless lists, he has some interesting pieces of wisdom."

"Sure, Tony, here it is," Karl said, tossing it to Tony. "Check out the figures I wrote in the back. Mother should still be alright, even with the new losses."

Tony sat near the fire, reading the ledger. The notes about the good horse dying brought an ache to his throat. He could read his father's pain in the pages.

Ruth came over and sat next to Tony. She nestled into his side and looked at the ledger with him. Karl had crawled into his blankets. He and Harry had the next watch. Tony and Haat would have the early morning watch.

"My goodness, Tony," Ruth said, "Your father had to carry a 150-pound pack, plus the heavy long rifle. That total must have weighed more than your father soaking wet."

Tony nodded. "Not to mention that he had not been eating very well. That is, until he met Don Sikes." Tony opened the ledger to the snow-covered cabin.

"This is where my father spent the winter. He spent his days talking with the dearly departed Don Sikes, bundled in a buffalo robe in a corner. He ate well that winter, thanks to the help of Don Sikes supplies."

"He would tell us the story of sending word to the Sikes family in Philadelphia. It was one of the first things he did after arriving in Elkader. It was called Pony Hollow back then. He writes of wanting it to be the first thing he did when he got back to civilization."

"He had gotten a letter back from the Sikes family six months later. It thanked him for letting them know what had happened to Don and for giving him a decent and Christian burial."

Ruth squeezed Tony's arm and gazed at the page showing a sketch of the cabin and Don Sikes' gravestone.

"Yes, Ruth, he had left the cabin a healthier and happier man. He had eaten well and improved his list of assets in his ledger."

"Wait a minute, Tony," Ruth said as she looked at the ledger. "Tell me how he increased his assets and decreased the weight of his pack. He estimated the pack was 110 pounds."

"I don't know, Ruth. He was lifting the pack and guessing the weight. Maybe he was in better shape and it made the pack easier to lift."

Tony turned the next few pages of the ledger. "Look here, Ruth. This is where he lost almost everything when his raft went over the falls." He traced his finger along his father's sketch of a falls.

It was time to turn in. Tony closed the ledger and slipped it into his saddle bag. He promised himself that he would look at Karl's figures the first thing in the morning.

Tony and Ruth walked over to the canvas tent that they had rigged just off from the chuck wagon. Karl had asked his brother why they bothered to build a tent every night. They could sleep in the chuck wagon. Smiling, Karl continued and said it even had springs for comfort. Another embarrassing moment for Tony.

Karl woke up just as the eastern sky began to get light. Poco had the fire going and a pot of coffee boiling. The aroma of coffee went a long way toward helping Karl climb out of the blankets.

Pouring a cup of coffee, he noticed fresh biscuits on the chuck wagon tailgate. Grabbing a couple, he dipped them into honey and sat down next to an oak tree to watch the sun come up. He could hear the cows waking up and moving out to graze. Tony was singing a Finnish lullaby that they had learned from their father.

Ruth came out of the tent and slowly stretched to get the kinks out of her back. Karl watched her in the early morning light. She had a light green gingham dress. Her shoulder-length blond hair was tied into two pigtails.

She had a way of moving that could get a man's attention, but Ruth only had eyes for Tony. She grabbed her apron from the back of the chuck wagon and slipped it on.

"Poco, I'll fill the water barrel before starting the porridge." Grabbing the water bucket, she pranced down to the stream.

He was turning away and scolding himself for looking when he heard Tony shout from the direction of the herd.

"Karl! Karl! I got it!" He was galloping his horse toward the camp.

Karl's heart had done a flip when he heard the shout. He was sure that it was Indians or something else bad. Standing with his legs spread, he watched Tony gallop up. Tony leaped from his horse and ran toward Karl, waving the ledger.

"Father hid the gold! I think he hid it," he said, his eyes wide with excitement.

Opening the ledger to the good horse's death, Tony pointed to the pack weight. He then turned to leaving the snow-covered cabin.

"You see, Karl, the pack was lighter. First, I thought the change was because he was in better shape. You and I both know that father was great at judging weight."

"Slow down, Tony. Now tell me what you are talking about and keep your voice down." Glancing around, Karl saw Josh was busy stowing his bedroll, Haat was with the cattle, and Poco was busy with Ruth at the chuck wagon.

"Last night, Ruth and I were reading father's ledger. She asked about how father could carry 150-pound packs plus his long rifle for any distance. She then noticed that father's pack when he left the cabin was only 110 pounds.

"Don't you see, Karl? He had more assets listed in the ledger, but his pack had gotten lighter. He must have left something behind. It had to be some of the gold."

"Don't get your hopes up, Tony. He may have left other things," Karl said as he reached for coffee mug. He noticed that his hand was shaking just a little.

"Karl, father never included money, his money belt, or the gold in his ledger. Mother said he was wearing the money belt filled with gold coins when he walked out of the Turkey River. Jacob Wolfe broke his wrist punching it." Tony's eyes were dancing with excitement in the morning light.

Karl sipped the coffee. It had gotten cold. "Let me think about this, Tony. Don't talk to anyone about it. I'll keep the ledger to study it."

It was too easy, the solution to their mother's money problem, that is. Karl did not believe it could be solved so simply. He stared at the ledger. What Tony had said made sense.

A couple weeks before his father died, he remembered a conversation between his father and mother. Father had wanted to take a trip west. Their mother had put her foot down and told him that he had almost died the last time. She wouldn't hear of it again.

They had talked late into the night. He had heard his mother crying softly and his father telling her that it had to be done and that he would be careful. The conversation could have been about going back for the hidden gold.

That night, Karl pulled Tony aside after supper. "I think you might be right on this, Tony. First, we got to get these cattle to Fort Dakota. Then we can send money back to mother. Just in case we don't find the gold, she will have something."

"Albert can bring it to her. We'll ask Haat to join us in the search. Remember, Tony, gold is a funny thing. It can make a good man turn bad. Let's keep this between us. Not even Ruth."

Tony nodded in agreement. "It won't be easy keeping it from Ruth, but I won't say a thing."

"Can I tell her in Fort Dakota before we head out?" Tony asked.

Karl smiled. "It would only be right to do so."

The rest of the drive to Fort Dakota went smoothly. They didn't lose any more cattle at night. They did give one of the older cows to three Indians they came across who were in need of meat for their women and children. Haat talked with them and learned about trouble spots they could avoid between there and the fort.

They arrived in early October. The leaves were a blaze of gold and red colors. One hill just east of the fort was covered with aspen, and they were a brilliant gold. There were clumps of dark green spruce trees within them that set the gold off even more.

Major Thomas was still waiting for orders. He gave them a victorious army's welcome as they drove the cattle to a pasture near the fort. Karl caught a glimpse of Karen standing within the shadow of the commissary.

He suddenly sat a bit straighter in the saddle. He gave quick instructions to the crew as they bunched the cattle for counting. He hoped that Karen had noticed.

"Run the cattle through the chute over there, please. We need to count and inspect them."

Karl looked toward the speaker and there stood Lieutenant Sparks.

"Why, lieutenant, I see you made first. The army can always recognize a good man."

Impatiently, the lieutenant replied, "Quickly, we need to get this finished. Dinner will be served shortly."

The count came out at 236 head, and the condition was marked down as good. Karl had not made any decision on the horses yet, so he figured that they could do that another day.

"Mr. August, the count came out with 207 head with the Circle A brand and 29 with the Leaning J brand. Can you show me a copy of the ownership papers, please?"

Karl thought, *What a polite man.* Digging out the ownership papers, he handed them to Lieutenant Sparks.

Looking them over, the lieutenant looked up. "Is Mr. James Wolfe here? He owns the Leaning J cattle."

Karl called Josh over. "Lieutenant, this is James's brother. James Wolfe was killed by Comanches during the drive."

"I'll need a transfer of ownership to you, Mr. August."

"Lieutenant, you don't understand. He was killed. Therefore, he could not give me a transfer of ownership." Karl could feel a slow burn coming on.

"Mr. August, I am sorry for any confusion. If two of the crew, not related to you, sign a document confirming that Josh here is in fact James's brother, then he can give you a transfer, or he can receive money for the Leaning J cattle."

Karl looked at Josh. Josh's face was pale and his brows were pinched.

"How much would the Leaning J cattle sell for?" Josh asked.

Karl looked at him with surprise. He then realized that Josh hadn't been part of the discussion Karl had had with James in Texas. It had been implied that the cattle would all be sold as a joint herd.

"We are paying $27 dollars a head. That would be. . ." the lieutenant said, doing some quick figuring on his paper, "a total of $783."

Josh hesitated a bit more. "Ah . . . no, of course, they are to be sold as a total herd to Karl here."

"Very well. I will make out two receivers for the cattle. One for 29 head with the Leaning J brand. And one for 207 with the Circle A brand. You then take them to the purser and he will give you the correct forms to transfer the Leaning J brand to Mr. August."

"Don't forget to have two of the unrelated crew sign the verification form that Josh is in fact James Wolfe's brother."

Filling out the receivers quickly, he handed one to Karl and the other to Josh. Karl looked at the total on his receiver, $5562 for the 206 head. Doing the math quickly in his head, he came up with a total of $6345.

"Hey captain, are you done with that sharp young lieutenant?" It was Major Thomas. "Let's go eat at Lou's. His wife is roasting elk tonight."

"We will be right along, major. We have to take care of our horses first."

The major walked with Karl as he led his horse to the stable. "Captain, I see you have an Indian and a black with you."

"Yes I do, major. The Indian is my brother and the black is a good friend. Will that be a problem?" Karl asked.

"It won't be at Lou's, captain. But in the fort, the Indian may be. As far as your black. . ."

"His name is Harry, major."

"Yes, as far as Harry, did you know we are enlisting blacks? I saw how Harry handled horses. The army could use his talents. Do you mind if I talk to him?"

"Not at all, major. He is his own man, so if what you offer appeals to him, it will be his decision."

"Great . . . great. Hand those reins over to the private and let's get some chow."

Tony walked up to them. "Hello, major. Good to see you again."

"You are Karl's brother, right?"

"Yes I am, major. My wife is over in the chuck wagon, and she wasn't feeling well this morning. Can you recommend any quarters for us?"

"Sure can, young man. Married, hey?" The major slapped Tony on the back.

"Right over there, the second building from the end is vacant. We just had an officer and his wife move east last week. Should have about everything you need in it. If your wife is able to eat, just go over to the commissary and they will put a basket of stuff together for you."

"Hey, Tony, send Poco over to Lou's. He can enjoy someone else's cooking for a change," Karl called out.

"Will do, Karl." Tony trotted back to the chuck wagon.

As they walked across the compound, heading for Lou's, Karl noticed that there were several new buildings and additional ones just getting started. They were expanding the fort.

They walked into the low building. The now familiar smell of cigars, sweat, and spilt rye filled their nostrils. Lou was behind the bar, with the same turkey neck and big ears.

"Welcome back, captain." Lou looked as Josh, Harry, Haat, and Albert followed Karl in. They stepped up to the bar and Lou grabbed a bottle, "Rye everyone?"

With drinks poured, the major made a toast. "Here's to old friends and new friends, and most important, good rye."

Poco walked in and reached for his glass of rye. "What was it we were drinking to?" he asked as he gulped down the rye.

They all sat down to enjoy Lou's wife's supper. The elk roast was sliced into thick slabs and was tender enough to cut with a fork. Her beans had a maple flavor to them, and she had hot cornbread with plenty of butter.

They ate the food, which was served with buttermilk. When the major suggested some more rye, Harry and Haat declined and excused themselves. They wanted to go back to the horses.

It was full dark, with a chill in the air, as Karl and the major walked out of Lou's. Fall was definitely in the air. Haat and Harry met them as they headed for the barracks.

"We figure that we best bed down in the chuck wagon, Karl," Harry said. "Haat and I would feel much more comfortable there."

Karl began to say something when the major placed his hand on his back.

"You have good men there, Karl. Like you said, they make their own decisions."

Karl stood outside the barracks, finishing his cigar. He was restless. He had missed spending time with Karen. The major had a way of making it difficult to leave. Now it was too late. Josh and Albert had turned in, looking forward to sleeping off the ground.

"Forget something, captain?"

Karl's breath caught momentarily when he heard the voice. Choking on the smoke, Karl coughed and turned to look at Karen. She was standing near a window with the light shining on her red hair.

"I always seem to surprise you, captain," she laughed.

He walked up to her quickly and it took all of his restraint not to take her in his arms.

"How have you been, Miss Thomas?" Karl asked awkwardly.

"I will tell you how I have been, Captain August. I have been stuck in this backwoods fort all summer, not knowing if you were dead or alive," she said with just the right amount of passion.

Karl looked at her and saw the glistening of tears in the corner of her eyes. He could not help himself. He took her into his arms and held her close. They held each other and talked in the crisp night air until late. Karen finally said that she had to go and gave him a kiss that warmed him right down to his frozen toes. He had a difficult time getting to sleep that night.

He awoke and noticed that it was already light outside. He could smell Karen's perfume on his coat as he slipped it on. Karl stopped for a moment and closed his eyes, remembering last night.

"Are you ready to go?" It was Josh. He had just come back from the latrine.

Karl and Josh walked in the crisp morning air, the frost-covered grass crunching under their boots.

The purser gave them a bored stare as they walked into his office. He handed Karl the verification paper. Evidently, Lieutenant Sparks had alerted the corporal.

The transactions went much smoother this time. Karl got enough cash to pay off the crew. He gave each an extra month's bonus. Their trip home from Fort Dakota would be longer and he felt that they deserved the money.

When Karl gave Josh the money James would have gotten so he could bring it back to Tate Wolfe, he was surprised by the boy's reply. "I am staying here with you and the others. You're going to look for more gold. I heard you whispering about it."

"Josh, we don't even know if any gold exists. The money from the cattle drive won't pay off the note. What Tony, Haat, and I are doing is a very long shot. In fact, the danger we will face might not even make the search worthwhile. There is no way I could put your fathers remaining son in that kind of danger."

"Your father needs you back in Elkader." While it hurt to continue, Karl said, "He has big plans and will need you at his side. I want you to take the money James earned back to your father and help him deal with the loss of your brother. When we get back to Elkader, Tony will tell you all about the search."

While Josh's face showed disappointment, Karl felt that he had gotten through to the boy. If they did find the gold, he decided that some type of share would be given to Josh. He had been with them from the start of the adventure and deserved something for all he had done, and what he had lost.

Poco offered to drive the chuck wagon to Elkader and bring Albert and Josh home. Albert would carry their mother's money in a $5,535 bank draft. Karl and Tony both wrote their mother letters, letting her know what they were doing. Neither mentioned Haat. They decided that it would be best done in person.

Tony had a tin type picture taken of him and Ruth. He sent it with his letter, along with the news that she would be a grandmother.

Harry decided to enlist in the Army for two years. He would be part of the "Buffalo Soldiers" as the blacks came to be called by the Indians. Karl gave him a horse so that he would have one for personal use. He sold 10 horses to the army for $45 each. This money would be used to equip them for the search and give Ruth enough until they returned.

Karen and Ruth had become instant friends. Karen introduced Ruth around and made sure that she had every need taken care of. Ruth getting pregnant was a surprise to Tony. Karl had never seen his brother so proud.

Karl and Karen, along with Tony and Ruth, dined each night in the visitor's dining room of the commissary. While Tony was gone, Ruth would stay as a guest of Karen Thomas.

CHAPTER 13

It was the third week of October, and the air was brisk and cold when the three brothers headed out in search of their father's gold. The Sioux were still creating problems in the area. The men were well-armed, and all could read sign and fight. They took a pack horse along to carry supplies.

Karl was wearing his army coat and riding the buckskin, Tony had his new deerskin coat and rode the grulla, and Haat had a leather coat with fringe on the sleeves. He rode a sorrel that he had traded for at the fort. They had all wore new woolen britches, long johns, and heavy wool socks.

Each of their saddle bags included sulfur matches, and flint with a striking steel. Haat didn't fully understand why Karl insisted that they take the flint, but he was adamant about it.

Karl looked at his two brothers. This felt so right to him.

They knew that their father had spent the winter near some mountains in the Black Hills. Haat believed that they were the Six Grandfathers. At least that was the name given to them by the Lakota Sioux.

Haat's tribe had ranged in that direction, looking for horses to steal or other items of value. They had talked of the mountains. The description and sketches in the ledger made them the best guess.

They rode directly west. Their father had traveled further north and west. They hoped to save time by striking directly toward the mountains. They estimated that it would take two weeks by horseback.

The crossing of the Missouri River went well. The river was down in the fall. The prairie was all around them, with clusters of trees along the waterways. The leaves had dropped from the trees and their naked branches stood as stark testaments to the winter to come.

Their meals consisted of jerky, beans, and hard biscuits. Haat would use his bow to shoot game whenever possible. Sitting around a small fire, with coffee boiling and the others nearby, gave Karl a secure feeling. He could only imagine what it must have been like for his father, alone and with limited supplies.

"What are you and Ruth going to name the baby?" Karl asked.

"I don't know. I suggested Oli if it's a boy. Ruth didn't say yes or no."

Haat laughed, "How about Nina-ua-naka if it's a girl?"

Tony soaked a piece of biscuit in his coffee. "It's going to be a big responsibility, raising a child. I was just a boy myself when we left Elkader."

"You have grown into a man I'm proud of, Tony. Father taught us to respect others and take care of ourselves. He taught these things by example and you've learned well."

Haat cleared his throat. "You were both very fortunate. We come from the same father, but my only knowledge of him came from the words of my mother. When I hear you talk of him, I feel I know him better. I ache inside because I cannot stand in front of him and see his approving eye."

A week out, they had their first snow. Karl rolled out of his blankets and looked at a world of white. Shaking the snow off his blankets, he pulled his socks and boots on. It was early for snow, and it should melt in the next day or so.

Karl decided to light their fire with a flint. Searching around, he found some dry tinder under a low bush. Assembling some dry sticks around the tinder, he began to strike the flint.

Tony raised up on one elbow. "What the heck are you doing? Look at the snow!"

Haat carefully moved his blankets over to keep the snow out. "Is the coffee ready yet?"

Tony piped up, "I noticed you have been drinking coffee lately."

"Even an Indian can be seduced by the evil brew," Haat snorted.

Breakfast was over quickly, and after brushing the snow from their horses they saddled up and headed west.

They were looking for a good place to eat the midday meal when Tony felt something grab at his hat, followed by the crack of a rifle. Looking back, they saw six Sioux riding hard toward them.

Spurring their horses, the three rode for some willows. The pack horse was staying right with them. Haat arrived at the willows first, leaped from his horse and started returning fire at the Sioux. Karl rode in and swung down from his horse. Slipping on the wet snow, he fell flat on his back.

Tony arrived last, closely followed by the pack horse, and slid to the ground. He ran back, expecting to find that Karl had been shot. He was glad to see that Karl was up and also returning fire.

It was pure luck that the willows were on the edge of a dry stream and had a natural bank around them that was defendable. One of the Sioux was knocked off his horse by a well- placed shot from Haat. The other five left their horses and started slowly crawling toward the willows.

Haat set his rifle down and took his knife from its sheath. He motioned that he was going to go out and circle them from the left. Tony hoped that he or Karl wouldn't mistake Haat for one of the Sioux.

It had been 20 minutes since Karl and Tony had last seen the Sioux. Their hands were cold and stiff from holding the rifles. The melting snow was working its way through their wool pants.

They had no idea where Haat was. Suddenly, there was a scream in the direction of the Indians that sent chills up both of their spines. Karl thought that he caught sight of movement to his right. One of the Sioux was moving down the dried stream.

A second scream was heard, this time more muffled. Karl was watching up the stream and again saw a shadow move. He squeezed off a shot in the direction of the movement. He heard a grunt and then the sound of someone retreating.

They lay in the willows for another half hour when they heard a clucking sound to their left. Tony strained his eyes for any movement.

"Don't shoot, brother!" Haat hissed.

Out of the shadows, Haat appeared and moved alongside them.

"How do you do that?" Tony asked.

"Practice," Haat replied. "I think the Sioux have moved out. They are down to three, and one of them you wounded, Karl."

Tony stared at their brother Haat. Their father would have been proud of him. Watching for any movement around them, they gathered the horses.

They rode two hours east before choosing a spot to eat their meal. Jerky, and dry biscuits with water from their canteens, were consumed in silence. They were cold from their damp clothing, but couldn't take a chance making a fire.

Two weeks to the day, they arrived near the Six Grandfather Mountains. Tony was the first to spot a cabin. Its roof was sagging, and one wall was toppling over. They rode up to the door and stopped short.

Lying halfway in the doorway was a badly decomposed body. Whoever the man was, his life had been cut short by the Sioux or Cheyenne. There were two arrows in his back. The man had been scalped and any weapons had been taken.

He had been dead for over two weeks. The cold weather had kept away the flies and other insects. The strong smell of man had kept wild animals at bay.

Haat and Tony rode in opposite directions around the cabin, checking the area. Karl stepped over the body to survey the cabin and stood in the low light, waiting for his eyes to adjust.

In the far corner to his right, he could see a bed. The leather supports had rotted and it sagged severely in the middle. He felt a tingle run through his body. He thought about the stories his father had told them.

Glancing at the near corner, he realized that might have been where Don Sikes had spent the winter. Slowly, he walked around the cabin, reliving the descriptions his father had told them. He ran his fingers through the ash in the fireplace.

The cabin was dust-covered. The air was musty, with the smell of decaying wood. Prior storms or heavy snow had taken a part of the roof off and rafters sagged down to the area of the collapsed wall. There was the odor of the dead man in the doorway. The mummification of the man had lessened the rotting smell. Karl ducked under a sagging rafter and sat on the bench next to the table. This would have been the same table where his father had eaten and written in his ledger.

Karl heard horses approaching the cabin. Removing his Army Colt from its holster, he walked to the edge of the door. He could see Haat and Tony. He slipped the revolver back into the holster and stepped out into the fresh air.

"We found his horse. It was killed a little way from the cabin." Haat was pointing to the west. "It looks like the horse collapsed during the chase. He then made it to the cabin, where he fell. He was no doubt hit with the arrows before he got to the doorway."

"I didn't find anything but father's recollections in the cabin. It was just like he had described, except for the collapsed wall and part of the roof coming down," Karl said, looking back at the cabin.

"We better take care of its last resident," Karl suggested. "Let's see if we can find Don Sikes' grave."

The three of them spread out, looking for the gravestone. "I found it," Tony called out.

He was standing just south of the cabin. The stone was covered with moss on the north side. They could still read the words chiseled into the stone by their father. Tony was running his fingers through the lettering when Karl and Haat walked up.

Karl remembered how his father had talked of stopping and saying a prayer over remote graves that he'd found. Karl knelt briefly and prayed.

Haat waited until Karl stood back up. "The animals have started tearing the horse apart. The saddle is still on the carcass. There is a name carved in the back of the saddle."

Together, Karl and Haat rode back to the horse. Tony chose to stay at the cabin and look around. They found the name and more on the saddle. There was also a town and state: Tim Cross, Spartanburg, SC

Karl and Haat rode back from the horse carcass, carrying the saddle. Tony was kneeling over the body. He was going through the pockets.

"There's nothing on the body but a pocket watch. His rotting britches are Confederate. Shirt was probably bought at a trading post. The watch cover has 'T.C.' engraved on it."

Taking the shovel from the pack horse, they began to dig the grave alongside Don Sikes'. Haat paused during the digging.

"Do you think our father would have buried the gold in the same grave as Don Sikes?"

"Not a chance," replied Karl. "Father was funny about graves. He would never do something that would require a grave to be dug up."

Haat handed the shovel to Karl. The digging continued until they had a good, deep grave. No animal would dig up Tim Cross.

Tony selected an acceptable stone to engrave 'Tim Cross 1866'. While Tony was making the stone, Karl and Haat searched the valley for any clues of the gold's location.

They looked for landmarks shown in their father's ledger. There was a cabin, the grave, mountains behind the cabin, and a lightning-struck tree stump that had been hit a few years ago. That could have been the tree in the sketch.

The burying of Tim Cross was complete, and the men stood around it with hats in hand. Tony said a brief prayer.

The cabin was not livable, so they set up a camp just to the south. The area didn't offer any good cover for the troop tent they'd gotten at the fort. From two directions, low brush offered some concealment. The canvas tent had low walls and a sloping roof. It would be cold at night and hot when the sun was shining. It would sleep the three of them and keep their supplies out of the weather.

Haat was up the next morning before the sun. After getting the fire going, he stuck his head into the tent.

"Karl, Tony, we have a problem. There was snow last night. We won't be able to see anything that would lead us to where father hid the gold."

Karl and Tony scrambled out of their blankets and joined Haat in front of the tent. The moon was full and large in the western sky. The ground was covered with a thin blanket of pure white snow.

Karl felt a sinking feeling. Time was running out, and if the snow came and stayed, they would not be able to search until spring. That would be too late to save their home.

Haat spent the day searching the valley. Tony did some hunting to supplement their food. Karl stayed at the camp and sat on a rock in front of the tent, studying the ledger for any clues leading to the gold.

The temperature was in the fifties. Snow was melting and Karl could see large patches of brown appearing. The front of the tent and around the fire had been trampled into dirty snow and mud. At noon, he went over to his buckskin and the pack horse and moved them onto better grass.

He took out the horse brush and gave both a good rubdown. Keeping busy helped him think. His father had made a few notes in the margins around his sketch. He had numbers near each landmark. The grave had a '0' near it.

Karl decided that the numbers were steps from the grave to each landmark. He paced the distance to the cabin from the grave, then to the tree stump. The number of steps seemed to be correct.

Oli had written on the bottom of the page: "Mr. Sikes is bathed in the glow." Next to it was a number that did not match any landmarks. It was larger than any other on the page. It could be that he'd just been figuring something. He'd been a detailed man.

Karl heard a single shot around mid-afternoon. It was toward the mountains. He said a quick prayer hoping that it was Tony shooting at game, and not being shot at.

Looking around, he knew that the tent was exposed from the west. It could be seen from across the valley. They had a clear area, which would prevent an enemy from getting too close, but they had nothing to hide behind to shield their position.

Karl justified it because they did not plan on being in the area long. Taking the time to set up a more defendable location was something they didn't have.

Haat rode in on his sorrel and walked up to the fire. He poured a cup of coffee and sat against an old pine stump. He was about to speak when they both heard Tony's horse trotting toward the camp. He had a small deer across the back of his saddle.

"We have fresh meat for dinner. I got it, so one of you can clean and cook it." He dropped the deer near the camp and rode his grulla to join the other horses.

Haat picked up the deer and hung it in a branch on a nearby oak. He quickly and deftly skinned and cut up the deer. He brought Karl several venison steaks to broil over the fire. While they sat by the fire and enjoyed the aroma of the sizzling steaks, they looked at the ledger.

"I think the number that doesn't make sense is the distance to the gold," Haat said, glancing at the grave.

Karl stood up and looked around. He could see Tony finishing rubbing down the grulla. If what the ledger said about "bathed in the glow" was correct, it had to be the glow of the sun. Or was it the golden glow?

"I am sure there is a reference to the east, south, or west," Karl said, looking to the south.

"I believe it's the distance from the grave. Father may have been worried about the landscape changing when he got back and included that to make sure he had a measurement to fall back on," Haat concluded.

Tony came back from rubbing his horse down and could smell the broiling meat. "I hope those steaks are done, because they smell good enough to eat raw."

The men sat and enjoyed the venison. Karl brought Tony up to date on what he and Haat had discussed.

Tony, being a practical thinker, said, "Tomorrow we make a big circle from the grave, at the distance of the number. We then look for any possible hiding places along the circle."

Karl had trouble sleeping that night. He felt that they were close to the gold. He knew that the notes in the ledger were for his father's benefit to relocate the gold, and not for others. He was sure that the grave was a key. Tomorrow morning, he would be at the grave before sunrise.

The next morning the air was crisp and cold. The ground was slightly frozen and stiff under Karl's boots. He made his way over to the grave site. The moon was setting in the west. The valley was bathed in its soft light.

The shadows made eerie figures across the landscape. A lone wolf howled in the night with a chilling sound. Karl got comfortable and lit a cigar. Slowly, the eastern sky began to get light. Karl watched the sun come up and he kept an eye on Don Sikes' grave stone. Nothing!

Other than a beautiful sunrise, no new information was found. Karl headed back toward the camp. Haat had a fire going and Tony was mixing biscuit dough. The Dutch oven was heating on the fire, and the coffee pot water was boiling. Haat poured a measured amount of grounds into the pot and gave them a quick stir to stop the foaming.

Soon, their breakfast of fried side meat and biscuits was over. Each man was busy cleaning up after breakfast and stowing supplies.

Tony, half-thinking out loud, asked, "I wonder if father set Don Sikes' stone so it faced the gold. Could that be the glow he was talking about?"

Karl slapped his knee. "You know, Tony, it does make sense."

"Thank you, Karl," Tony smiled. "Now we won't need a circle, just part of one."

They walked the paces equivalent to the number on the bottom of the page. They made several trips, creating an arc. Following the arc, each looked for places that their father might have chosen. Passing the lightning-struck tree, they looked back at the grave. This might be the place. Continuing, they found a rock ledge. There was dirt and rocks along it, but nothing obvious. Once again, they looked back at the grave. Again, the direction was possible.

They spent the morning choosing probable hiding places. The plan was to investigate closer after the midday meal. The rest of the venison had been put into the Dutch oven with molasses and a few other seasonings. Adding some water so that it wouldn't burn, they had left it to cook.

At noon, they sat around the Dutch oven, dipping biscuits into the tender juicy meat. Haat finished up first and went back to look at the selected sites. Karl and Tony watched him slowly work his way around. He turned suddenly and jogged back to the fire.

"I think I have found the spot," Haat said, taking one more biscuit and dipping it into the meat.

"How do you know?" Karl asked.

"There are some rocks in front of the ledge that were not placed by nature. They may have been placed by our father. Stones that lay eventually weather, and sharp edges wear and weather on the top. Some of these stones are more weathered on the bottom than on top. They were carefully placed there to look natural."

Quickly, they cleaned up from the midday meal, and with shovels in hand they went to the rock ledge. Haat had placed two sticks about 30 feet apart. Rocks, dirt, and part of the rotting tree lay along the front of the ledge.

"Where do we want to start digging?" Tony asked.

"I got an idea," Karl said. "You two stand to each side of the ledge. I am going back to the grave stone to fire a rifle squarely from the front of the stone."

Hurrying back to the tent, Karl took his Henry rifle and he selected a long, straight stick, about eight feet. Returning to the grave stone, he carefully laid the stick square in front of the stone. Crouching behind the grave stone, Karl sighted down the stick toward the stone ledge. He could see Haat and Tony standing on each end.

Karl squeezed off a shot. The Henry rifle jumped in his hands. The report of the shot echoed off the mountains behind. Karl stood and looked at the ledge. The line he sighted down favored the tree stump side of the ledge.

Haat ran forward and stopped along the ledge. He had picked out the spot where the bullet had hit. Karl and Tony joined Haat, and together they began to remove stones and dirt. Part of the tree lay in the way. Tony returned to the camp and got an axe. The section of the rotting tree was removed. By dusk, they had a section of about six feet cleared away.

Leaving the shovels at the ledge, they went back to the camp. Tony built up the fire while Haat went to water the horses and move them to fresh grass. Karl walked back to the grave stone and looked down at where they had dug. He felt that they were digging in the right direction. That is, if the gold was hidden in front of the ledge.

So far, they were removing everything to bare ledge. They were confident that the gold was under the rock and dirt and not buried deeper. They hoped that their assessment was correct.

Thickening clouds were building up in the west. The wind was cold. After dinner, they sat in the tent and cleaned their guns in lantern light. The wind was buffeting the tent. Karl removed the derringer from his vest pocket and cleaned it.

"Where did you get the little gun?" Haat asked.

"I got it off a thug on the pier in St. Louis," Karl replied.

"Why haven't we seen it before?"

"That is because it is a sneak gun. If everyone knows you have it, it can't be a sneak gun," Karl answered in a matter-of-fact tone.

Tony chuckled as Haat grunted and shook his head.

They woke to a snow storm. It was not a blizzard, but it was close. The snow was blinding and felt like needles hitting their faces.

"We best get the horses closer into camp," Karl yelled over the sound of the wind.

They could barely see the outline of the horses standing, heads down, with the storm to their backs. Haat ran to get the horses. He came back leading three. The pack horse was gone.

They brought the horses to the cabin and tied them along the downwind side. The cabin would offer a wind break. They went to the tent and hunkered down, trying to keep warm. They made a meal of cold biscuits and jerky. Attempts to make a fire did not work in the open area. Their canteens were mostly frozen and offered little to drink.

Shivering, they grabbed their blankets and a few other items, abandoned the tent and headed for the cabin. The ground was frozen and the wind kept it blown clear. Entering the cabin, Karl took the door that had fallen from its brittle leather hinges. Propping it up against the opening, he motioned Tony to slide the table against it. The wind-blown snow continued to swirl inside the decaying structure.

Haat was busy at the fireplace, putting a stack of kindling together which he had found. Tony got their lantern lit and shed some light. Slowly, the flames began to curl around the kindling. With the help of the lantern light, they were able to collect up other pieces of wood. There was a small stack near the fireplace. No doubt left by one of the many visitors that had stayed in the cabin since there grandfather. It was punky, but dry.

The opening in the roof was away from the fireplace. It allowed the wind to blow into the cabin and made the cold fireplace chimney a poor draft for the fire. More than a little of the smoke went into the cabin. Fortunately, it did not stay long and exited though the roof.

Wind and snow blew in through the poorly chinked logs. The sagging rafters shook and the door rattled against the opening. They were all thankful that the collapsed wall was not on the windward side.

Karl filled the coffee pot with snow that had drifted into the corner. Momentarily, he thought about Don Sikes. Shaking his head, he returned and put the coffee pot next to the smoldering fire.

Slowly, the chimney warmed up and the smoke chose that route over the hole in the cabin roof. The three sat around the fireplace with their blankets over their backs. The fire offered some heat on one side of the men. By continuing to turn they warmed all sides. Soon, the water in the coffee pot was boiling. Haat measured the coffee grounds into the pot. Tony and Karl couldn't say why, but Haat's coffee tasted the best.

Tony put a pot of beans on to cook. It was barely midday and the storm was still howling outside. They sat watching the pot slowly come to a boil. Each was with his own thoughts, although all three wanted to believed that they were close to finding the gold. They needed to finish up here and head back to the fort, with or without the gold, in the next day or so. They did not want to get trapped in deep drifts. A lengthy freeze would make it impossible to dig at the ledge.

Doubt began to creep into Karl's thoughts. It was only a guess that the gold was near the ledge. The existence of the gold was also a guess from what was in the ledger. Before the snow started, he had felt hope and was confident that they were correct in their figuring. He now felt cold, hungry, and the prospect of finding the gold seemed remote.

As the pot of beans began to slowly bubble, Haat sliced some side meat into the pot and poured some molasses in from a tin that had been warming next to the fire. After putting a measure of salt in, he gave it a couple of stirs and sat back.

Slowly, the smell of the cooking beans brought them to life. Tony filled everyone's cup with more hot coffee. With the fire in front, blankets on their back, and a hot cup of coffee to warm their hands, they were almost feeling human again.

Tony blew on his cup and sipped the coffee. "I think we are on the right track. Father did everything but put an 'X' on the sketch. He couldn't have made it clearer."

Haat nodded. "The rocks and dirt we are moving were put there by someone, and not by nature. He put a wide pile to make sure the place was not obvious."

Karl stirred the beans and sat back. "I wish I had the same confidence that you both have. As soon as the storm is over, we will try and dig. We have three more days and we have to head back. If we don't, we can't make it back to Elkader before the note is due."

Karl's comments put a damper on the group and they quietly stared at the bean pot.

Morning brought new hope. The storm was gone and little snow remained on the windswept, frozen ground. The sun was bright. Tony fried side meat for breakfast and they dipped cold biscuits into the grease. Using their knives, they speared strips of the crisp meat from the frying pan and ate them. The hot coffee was good and strong.

The horses had huddled close to the cabin, keeping out of the wind, and had come though the storm well. Tony led them to some dry, brown grass. It was plentiful and would make good grazing. Walking back from picketing the horses, he noticed that their tent had blown down.

They returned to the ledge and took up their shovels. Some snow had blown against the ledge, filling in the area they had already dug and covering the rest of the stone and dirt in a foot and a half snow drift. The snow had prevented the stones and dirt from freezing solid.

By noon, the men had stripped their coats and had dug another five feet. In full agreement, they decided to continue digging rather than eating. The sun set early and they wanted to dig as much as possible.

An hour later, they hit a recess in the stone ledge. It was waist-high and as the digging continued down the ledge, it measured three-feet wide. With chaffed hands and broken nails, slowly the rocks were removed from the depression. Excitement began to build inside each man as the indentation yielded more rocks and began to look like it could be a cave.

Their hands and feet were cold. Grasping the rocks with numbed fingers was difficult.

"You know that father filled this opening in spring weather. That is, if this is the hiding place," Tony said, grunting as he passed a large stone to Karl.

"No pessimism, brother. This has to be it, or we are out of time."

Afternoon saw the temperatures back below freezing. None of the three noticed. They were all working fast and sweating. Karl had cautioned them over the danger of sweating in freezing temperatures, but none could help themselves. They felt that they were so close.

Suddenly, the stones gave way to a cave. It took only a few minutes to widen the opening so that they could crawl in. The cave was dark and they could not see anything. The sun was getting low in the western sky. Haat ran back to the cabin and got the lantern.

Karl lit the lantern and took a moment to appreciate the heat that it gave off. He then crawled into the cave. It was about 15 feet deep. Close behind him were Tony and Haat. It widened a bit at the end, so the three could kneel shoulder-to-shoulder.

The light fell on glistening gold. The three brothers froze in place, unable to speak. In front of them were three neatly piled stacks of gold coins and some small bars. Under one of the bars was a piece of paper.

Karl noticed a hand print in the dust. Pointing it out to his brothers, he carefully placed his hand over the print. In turn, Tony and Haat did the same. Years ago, their father had knelt in this very spot when giving up this gold.

They began to shiver, partly from the discovery, but mostly from their sweaty shirts. It was their damp shirts that suddenly got Karl's attention. This gold would do nobody any good if they caught a chill and died of exposure.

"I don't know about you guys, but I am getting cold. We need to go back to the cabin and change into fresh shirts. We can build a fire and warm up a bit. We also have to move the horses near the cabin," Karl reminded them as he began to back out of the cave.

Haat and Tony waited a moment more inside the cave before they came out. Putting his coat back on, Karl headed for the horses before going to the cabin. He smiled as he saw the three horses contentedly grazing.

Karl entered the cabin and saw Haat starting the fire. Tony was wrapped in his blanket, shivering. Karl rubbed Tony's shoulders.

"As soon as we warm up a bit and get supper on the fire, we will take our saddlebags to the cave and put one stack in each set of bags."

Through chattering teeth Tony asked, "Why did he make three equal stacks? Did he have a premonition that three sons would find the gold?"

"It is not likely, but it is a nice thought, Tony," Karl said, looking at Haat, who was watching him for an answer.

Karl knew that gold was selling for just under $30 per ounce. He had seen 100 pounds of gold before, during a shipment for the Army. This gold was almost as much. That would make the value over $40,000. It was more than enough to satisfy the note.

It took an hour for the three of them to warm up as darkness set in. It was a nervous, pins and needles hour. They had to fight the urge to run back to the cave and make sure that they were not mistaken in what they'd seen.

Walking with the lantern light to guide them, they went back to the cave and crawled in. Now that they were properly dressed in dry clothes, the lantern heat was almost too much in the cave. Karl lifted the bar off the paper and carefully put it into his pocket. Then he slowly transferred the stacks to the three saddlebags. A slow, final look told them that they had all of the coins and bars. One at a time, they crawled backwards out of the cave, dragging their saddlebags.

They returned to the cabin and sat in front of the fireplace. The bean pot was cheerfully bubbling with the promise of tender beans for supper. Suddenly, the three began to laugh and slap each other on the backs. The tension of the past few days drained away, and was replaced by pure joy.

Karl removed the paper that they had found in the cave. The paper had come from a back page of the ledger. It was a letter written by their father. Karl marveled at the clear, precise hand writing:

To the person who finds this gold.

My name is Olavi August. The year is 1840. This gold is legal Spanish treasure. Its location was told to me by my good friend, Jolly. It was found near the mountains of the West. I carried it with the help of a good horse for all these miles. I thought it would change my life. It was almost my death. At one time I would have carried it rather than food if the weight of both became too much.

Gold can be a good thing. It should be used to build and make your life better as well as those around you. It is my hope to come back and get this gold at a later time. You're finding it means that it did not happen.

Before you leave, do me these favors. Say a prayer over the grave of Don Sikes. If you get back east, send a message to Philadelphia and tell them that he died bravely.

In a few days I will be walking east to find my future. I hope to meet a woman who will stand by me and that I can grow old with. I have dreamt of strong sons and daughters to give me many grandchildren.

If by chance you are my sons that will mean, I was not able to make the trip with you. Take this gold back to your homes and use it for good. Your father has tested drink and wild living. It leaves you with a sore head and empty money belt.

Most Sincerely, Oli

Karl carefully folded the paper and placed it inside the ledger. Their mother would want to read this. He put his arms around his two brothers.

CHAPTER 14

That evening was spent sorting and cataloging the gold. Karl used a back page of the ledger to make the list. It was decided that each man would carry one-third of the gold. Once they reached the fort it could be divided again with a share for each and the rest to their mother.

Winter was doing its best to set in, and the two-week trip back to Fort Dakota would have its share of dangers. A blizzard could snow them in, even freeze them. Without the pack horse they had to discard some of the items, such as the tent, shovels, and some of the cook pans. Even the lantern would be left behind.

The next morning, Haat found the pack horse dead about a mile from the cabin. Wolves had stripped most of the meat from its bones. They often heard the long howls of the wolves at night. Karl would repeat the stories that their father had told about being chased by wolves and about turning on them and making meals from their meat.

It was time to head back. Karl stood for a long moment at the cabin door, leaning against the wall. Haat and Tony sat on their horses and waited.

"This was the very door that father burst through with the wolves at his back. It was the home of Don Sikes that kept father safe through the winter. It is the same cabin that kept most of the storm out and protected his three sons," Karl said.

He swung onto the buckskin and said, "Let's go home, brothers."

They rode for a while and Tony was deep in thought. "He didn't think he would ever come out of the wilderness, did he, Karl?" Tony asked. "Father mentioned getting the word to Don's people."

"When you think about it, Tony, he had many more miles to go than we do. He was alone, with war parties looking for opportunities."

The valley was frozen, with patches of snow. The bright sun was warm on their faces. The three brothers would forever have this link to their father.

Tony sang a Finnish ballad about returning home as they slowly rode out of the valley, leaving the very important cabin behind.

The first week brought them half the distance to the fort. They had wanted to retrace the route that their father had taken, but time wouldn't allow it. Maybe another time, they decided.

Haat took on the responsibility of hunting for meat. One night they ate turkey, another was rabbit. All were taken with his bow.

On the morning of the eighth day, the sun was shining and they had gotten three inches of snow during the night. Tony suddenly motioned them to be quiet. He reached back for the Good Knife and his arm flashed forward, sending the knife into a roosting partridge. Another was sitting just above the downed bird. Haat sent an arrow through it. The birds made an excellent supper.

They arrived at the Missouri River on an unusually warm day. Snow was dripping from the trees. They could hear flocks of ducks on the river. Haat went downriver after the ducks, promising to be back by supper. Karl and Tony waded their horses across the river.

"Is that smoke?" Tony asked, pointing just up the bank to the other side.

"I believe it is, Tony. It is in the same area as the empty cabin we saw while going west."

It appeared that the occupant of the cabin had returned, and no doubt could offer them some hot coffee. Slowly approaching the cabin, the brothers looked for any possible trouble. They could see a horse tied in a lean-to on the side of the cabin. It had a brand that they had seen at the fort.

"Hello, the cabin!" Karl called out.

Slowly, the door opened, exposing a rifle barrel first. The man inside looked out through the crack in the door. Suddenly, it swung open and out stepped Josh.

"Hello, boys, I was hoping you would come by."

Tony swung down from the grulla and walked out extending his hand. "I thought you would be back in Elkader by now."

"I just couldn't leave without my friends. Where is Haat?"

"He went downriver to catch us some ducks for dinner."

Karl dismounted and walked the two horses near the lean-to and tied them to a rail. Walking back, he thought about his last discussion with Josh. He wondered if this was as good a time to let the boy know about his share.

"Come on in and have some coffee. I just finished making a pot."

"Are you alone out here?" Karl asked.

"Yes, I am. I got tired of sitting around at the fort. One of the soldiers told me about this cabin and he figured you would come by here."

Josh pulled out two stools for them.

"Get out of them heavy coats and all that hardware and have a seat. I will whip up some fresh cornbread to go with supper. Ducks and cornbread sound mighty good," Josh said as he walked to the stove.

Karl and Tony hung their coats on pegs driven into the wall. The cabin was small and sparsely furnished. The hand-made table had four stools. There was a stand in the corner that had a basin on it. It would serve for food preparation, or a wash stand. Two bunks were built against the opposite wall. An impressive cook stove was near the wall, across from the bunks. You didn't see many of those in the wilderness.

They sat down and accepted the coffee from Josh. Karl looked up at the boy, "We had talked about you going back to Elkader to be with your family, to help your father with his grief over losing James."

Josh turned back to the stove and set the pot down. He turned back to the brothers with a gun in his hand. "That is what you would have liked me to do."

Tony was startled. "Put the gun down before you hurt someone, Josh."

Josh had a strange, wild look on his face. "You got the gold on the horses, don't you? You wouldn't be back yet if you hadn't found it."

"Hold on now, Josh. We found some. We talked of giving you a share. Now listen to Tony and put the gun down," Karl urged.

"I don't want no share," Josh snorted. "I'm taking it all."

"Josh, it is me, Tony, your friend," the younger August said.

"I was your friend, but I saw what you really were when you met Ruth. And then you decide to look for gold and wanted to cut me out of that too," Josh sneered.

"Take the guns out of your holsters and toss them away," he ordered. Karl and Tony did as he asked, hoping to reason with the confused boy.

"My father sent me with you to make sure you didn't succeed in bringing a herd to market. I got Sid and Ray to take the horse money. I killed Ray because he was going to tell you. James was supposed to stop you in St. Louis. Get your money and rough you up. He was strong, but dumb. He messed that up. He had a weakness for the bottle."

"That was where it was supposed to end. Broke, we were supposed to head back to Elkader. James and I decided we would continue and stop you in Texas. You know how that went. Then he had to get himself killed by the Commanches. Some friend you were, Tony. Once you met Ruth, I was just in your way."

"The worst part is you sent me home while you went to find the gold." Josh said, his voice breaking. Clearing his throat, he continued. "I told Poco and Albert I wanted to bring a stone down to James's grave. They believed me and left. I had supplies ready and got a horse. I came to this cabin and just waited."

Karl looked at Tony's face. It wore a look of pure shock. Josh, who had been his friend, had turned on him. And now he would likely kill him.

"You won't get away with this, Josh," Karl said, trying to reason with the young man. "Haat will come back soon and wonder what happened to us."

Josh smiled a cold smile. "I will let him walk in the door and put a bullet through him before he knows what hit him."

Josh had been swinging the Navy Colt back and forth between Tony and Karl. Karl watched as Tony continued to try and convince Josh to put down the gun. He noticed that Tony was using his hands to make his point. He was going for the Good Knife!

Karl could not let his brother kill the man who had been his boyhood friend. "The gold *is* outside on the horses, Josh." As the boy's eyes went to the window, Karl slipped the derringer out of the vest pocket, he brought it up just above the table and fired both barrels into Josh's chest.

Shocked by the gunshots, Josh's eyes opened wide and he tried to speak. The Navy Colt slipped from his fingers and he sank to his knees. Tony quickly moved to Josh and lowered him to the floor, cradling his head.

"Why? Josh, why?" Tony asked, tears running from his eyes.

Josh's head wobbled back and forth. "Just the gold, Tony. I wanted the gold." Josh coughed and flecks of blood spattered on his shirt. He shuddered and quit breathing. Tony lowered his head to the floor.

Karl collected the guns and took their coats from the pegs on the wall. Tony stood up, his face twisted with emotion. "Let's get out of here, Karl." Tony picked up a lantern as they left the cabin and smashed it on the floor. Flames leaped up along the wall.

They untied the horses and took Josh's horse and saddle. Slowly, they rode down the river as the cabin went up in flames behind them.

"What Josh did wasn't you fault," Karl told his brother.

"Gold can be a very bad thing for some people," Tony mumbled.

Haat came up the river, waving and holding up three ducks.

The remaining days riding to the fort were somber. Tony had lost a boyhood friend. Many of the problems on the drive became clear. Haat and Karl realized that James was the weaker one and Tate had given the responsibility of stopping the drive to Josh.

The fort came into view on the 22nd of November. The ground was covered with six inches of snow. The afternoon was bright. The stark contrast of the buildings against the background of the white snow was a pleasing sight.

Tony galloped ahead to find Ruth. It was the first smile that they had seen on him since the meeting with Josh. Haat and Karl rode toward the stable.

"See you found the missing horse." It was Lieutenant Sparks. "That horse flesh cost the Army $50 and we can't afford to lose them." He reached for the lead rope.

Karl handed the rope to the lieutenant. "You're welcome," Karl said as he rode past.

They handed their horses' reins to the young private in the stable and pulled the saddle bags off.

"Our horses have come a far piece. Can you give them some extra oats and a good rubdown?"

"Sure thing, captain" the private said as he led the horses inside.

Haat chuckled, "Once a captain, always a captain."

Karl saw Tony's horse tied in front of Karen's quarters and he was holding Ruth in his arms. Karen was leaning against the door jamb, watching Karl walk up.

"I'll be right with you, Haat. I'll meet you at Lou's for a drink after I say hello."

Haat handed Karl his saddlebags and snorted, "I'd be mighty drunk by the time you got there."

Karen held back as Karl got closer. "Are you going to always be running off someplace after we are married?"

Karl dropped the saddlebags onto the ground. Her stern face suddenly softened and she came into his arms. She looked up with tears on her cheeks. "I was so worried."

Karl kissed her softly and whispered, "All I want to do is stay close to you from now on."

"Hey there, Captain August." It was Major Thomas. "Finish up saying your hellos and let's go down to Lou's for a drink before supper."

Karen's face became stern again, but Karl knew that it was not real. "Uncle, you go down for just one drink and then get back here so Karl can clean up for dinner."

"Yes, niece. Come on, Karl."

Karl handed the saddle bags to Tony so that he could store them in the girl's quarters. His brother had no intention of leaving Ruth right now and together they walked into the quarters, Tony weighted down with three sets of saddlebags.

Haat joined them as the major and Karl walked into Lou's. Lou bobbed his head on his turkey neck and set them up with three ryes.

"You be here for supper?" Lou asked. "The missus has a ham in the oven."

"Not tonight, Lou," the major said. "These men are my guests for sup . . . ah, dinner."

Lou poured them another drink and the major offered cigars. Karl accepted and Haat declined.

"Someday you will have to tell me about the trip to the Black Hills. I noticed you brought the horse back that was stolen." The major took a long drag on the cigar.

The three of them walked back toward the ladies' quarters.

"I got you, Haat, and Tony quarters next to the ladies. Sorry, I couldn't get one for Tony and Ruth alone. I believe there are clean clothes in there for you. Dinner is at six sharp."

The major walked away to get ready for the evening meal. He puffed on the cigar, blowing smoke rings into the cool evening air. They found Tony already getting dressed. A private was waiting to take their boots.

The three brothers felt uncomfortable as they walked to meet the ladies. They were wearing stiff white shirts, dark Spanish-style wool pants, and their boots had been polished while they'd washed and shaved. Each had been given a heavy green wool coat with some silver trim on the lapels and cuffs. No doubt they were the spoils of some battle some time back.

Tony knocked on the ladies' door. Karen led the way, looking beautiful in her full dress. Both women had warm, wool shawls over their shoulders. They looked at the three men and both girls began to giggle.

Blushing, Karl said, "The clothes were not our idea. It's what was given to us."

"No, you don't understand," Karen said. "We think you men look great. It is just the change was more than expected."

Tony and Karl took their ladies by the arm, and with Haat walking alongside, they headed for dinner. It was a grand affair. The table was set with crystal and silver. There were crisply folded napkins at each setting. Everyone sat and made small talk while three privates hovered around, pouring the wine and bringing in each course.

Karl recognized two of them from his first meeting with Karen. Karen kept squeezing Karl's hand as they sat next to each other. Dessert was a cake with a crunchy white frosting. Karl noticed that Haat seemed right at home. No doubt it was from his time with the monks.

Karl had been at a couple of these types of dinners during the war. He had always felt that they were a waste of scarce resources. Karen seemed to enjoy them. He would keep his feeling to himself.

After dinner, the men retired to smoke cigars and sip brandy in a drawing room of sorts. The ladies sat together in another room and chatted about fashions and such. Karl noticed Tony glancing at Ruth through the doorway now and then.

After dinner was over, the three brothers and Ruth and Karen went back to their quarters. Haat tapped Karl on the shoulder.

"Don't you think we should go and check on that horse we brought in? Lieutenant Sparks had some concerns about it."

Karl was slow to catch on, but after some meaningful glances from Haat he came around. "You are right, Haat. I almost forgot. Forgive me ladies, Tony. Haat and I will be gone for about two hours."

"Want me to go with you?" Tony asked.

Karl gave him a stern look. "You best stay here alone and watch the saddlebags. Miss Karen, I'll see you in the morning."

With that, Haat and Karl walked to the stable. Sitting on a bench just inside the door, Karl continued to smoke his cigar. Haat took out his knife and began to whittle a piece of stick. They heard a crunch on the snow outside the door.

"I thought you men might need some coffee while checking that horse," Karen said, walking into the barn carrying a coffee pot and three tin cups. The three of them burst into laughter.

The morning was overcast, and busy. They decided how the gold would be divided. The gold weighed 93.5. pounds. It was selling at $28.26 per ounce. The purser offered to convert part or all of it to cash.

Haat wanted to keep his as gold. They decided that 15 pounds would go to each descendant of their father. That would include Jenny. The rest would be split between Haat's mother and Karl and Tony's mother.

With the money from the cattle sale and their mother's share, she would have more than enough to pay off the note. Now, the only problem was getting to Elkader before the end of November.

The major came up with the solution. He had finally received orders to go to Washington. It would be dinner parties and politics, but he was ready for the change from frontier life. He offered to provide an escort for Karen and Ruth to Elkader. He wanted to attend the wedding.

He got four fresh horses for Karl and Tony to ride. They should make Elkader in less than a week. That would be a day or two to spare. The major would bring their personal horses with him to Elkader.

Karl kept enough gold to pay off the note. The rest of the money would be coming with the escort.

Haat got his sorrel and bought another pack horse to carry items back to his village. His face was long as he looked at his brothers.

"It had been a lifelong dream of my mother and me that I could meet other sons of my father. I could not have asked for more brave or more honest brothers. Will we meet again?"

"Haat, we will not only meet again, but we will have more adventures," Karl said. "Once Karen gets tired of me being under foot, she will be happy to send me out. We can meet and follow our father's route from the Black Mountains."

Haat waved as he rode away. He would have many stories to tell around the winter fires. Karl and Tony sat on their horses until Haat rode from view.

"Aren't you going already? You have a wedding to plan," Karen called from the front of her quarters.

Smiling and waving, Karl and Tony turned their horses east.

CHAPTER 15

With threatening skies, Karl and Tony rode hard, each leading a spare horse behind them. There was eight inches of soft snow, which was no trouble for the horses. Karl was sure that they were running in front of a storm. They couldn't afford to stop. Tony figured that they could make 60 miles per day, and that would take just over five days for the trip.

Once, during the second day, three Indians rode out onto the trail and chased them. As it happened, Karl and Tony were on fresh horses and easily outran them. When the Indians pulled up, they'd given out shrill yells to spur their quarry on.

The night of the third day, they had just settled down when the snarls of a wildcat reached their ears. The horses stomped nervously, so they mounted back up and rode for another few hours. They then slept for five hours. As the sun came up with a flaming red sky, the horses were saddled and ready to go.

Tightening the cinch, Karl turned to Tony. "Smells like snow in the air."

"Let's hope it is just a dusting," Tony said.

By noon, the snow was coming down heavy. They had to slow down to prevent the horses from having a misstep. Their hats were pulled low over their eyes, neckerchiefs covering their faces. The horses had trouble with snow and ice building up around their eyes.

Karl pulled off under a stand of pine. The trees kept the snow off them while they gave the horses a breather. Wiping the snow from the horse's eyes and off their backs gave them some relief. Both Tony and Karl shook themselves off to remove the snow from their clothes. The snow that went down their necks slowly melted.

Tony built a small fire and made a pot of coffee. Karl took a sip and shook his head.

"I don't know what Haat does to coffee, but somehow it just tastes better."

"I agree, Karl. He has the knack for making coffee."

After soaking some hard biscuits in the coffee and chewing some jerky, they were ready to face the storm again. Switching the saddles to the extra horses, they rode out of the pines and spent a few minutes figuring the correct direction.

"The snow was sticking to the west side of the trees all morning. I don't think the wind direction changed," Karl said.

They moved out in an easterly direction. Karl's stomach was tight. The last thing that they needed was a snow storm. He knew that they wouldn't make more than 20 miles today. Three times that was needed to get home before the note was due.

If there were two more miserable souls, Karl had never seen them. The temperature was just below freezing and the flakes were big, thick, and stuck to everything. The only saving grace was there was no wind. Wind would have stopped them on the spot. It was getting too dark to be sure of their trail when Tony noticed a dim light to their left.

The light was coming from the trading post where they had stopped at he start of the trip. Tying their horses to the branches of a spruce tree, Tony followed Karl toward the log building.

"I would recommend taking our coffee cups in to drink out of," Tony said, remembering their first visit.

They walked into the trading post and had to take a moment to get accustomed to the light. The proprietor had a lantern burning near the door, which kept the back part of the room in the dark.

"Welcome back, boys." They looked at the toothless smile of the old man. His hair was still plastered to his scalp.

"We'll have a bottle of the good stuff and some coffee," Karl said.

The old proprietor brought a bottle with two cloudy glasses. They showed him their coffee cups and he went to the potbelly stove and got the coffee pot and filled their cups.

"I got cups, so you don't have to bring yours." The old man looked hurt.

Ignoring him, Tony asked, "Can you rustle us something to eat?"

The old man seemed to perk up. "We got some fresh bread, cheese, some stew on the back of the stove, or I could slice a couple steaks of the hunch of venison in the back room."

In unison, Karl and Tony said, "Bread and cheese, please."

"We need a place to spend the night and put four horses up," Karl said.

"You be welcome to sleep in front of the stove there. There is a lean-to against the back of this building that would hold four horses. Some hay on the far wall. Only cost you $4."

"Does that include the bread and cheese?" Tony asked.

"Sure does, but not the bottle." The old man flashed them another toothless grin.

Karl told Tony to stay and guard their cups while he went out and tended to the horses. The lean-to did hold four horses, but just barely. Karl put the feedbags onto the horses with the oats that they carried. He then rubbed down the horses with an old burlap bag he'd found. After they were done with the oats, he gave them each a good helping of hay.

Squeezing past the horses near the door, he hurried around the building to the front door.

Tony was sitting at the table with his feet up, eating a thick slice of cheese between two thick slices of dark bread. He had put extra cheese in his pocket. Karl brushed the snow off his head and shoulders. Sitting down across from Tony, he took out his knife and reached for the bread and cheese.

"You are going to like the bread, Karl. He put molasses in it."

Tony was right, the bread was very good. And the cheese was also aged just right. Karl decided that he would have to rethink his views on this place.

Karl poured some whisky into his coffee. Taking a big bite of bread and cheese, he washed it down with the coffee. For just a moment, all was right with the world.

After finishing their supper, Karl invited the old proprietor to join them. Smiling he grabbed a glass and sat down and poured himself a drink.

"How long does it take to get to Elkader from here?" Karl asked.

"Regular riding would take just over three days. I heared that a fella made it in two days of hard riding once. Course, it weren't snowing." Finishing the first, he poured another drink and drank it down.

He was reaching for the bottle again when Karl's hand stopped him. "How much do you want for the bearskin behind the bar?"

"Ain't for sale. Kind of my good luck hide, that one is." He took the bottle and poured his third drink.

Karl removed a gold coin from his money belt. "Would this pay for the bearskin and our stay?"

The old man's eyes opened wide. "I should say it would. Even the extra he put in his pocket." Taking the gold coin, he rubbed it between his fingers and bit down on it with some teeth he found in the back of his mouth.

"Told you that bearskin brung me luck." Tossing the coin into the air, he then slipped it into his pocket.

"We best sleep with one eye open tonight, Karl. He noticed where you got the coin."

Karl nodded, "He even noticed whatever you put in your pocket." He poured himself another drink. Having the bearskin would be worth it.

If the old man thought about trying for more gold coins, he'd obviously changed his mind. Both men got their first good night's sleep since leaving the fort.

It was still dark when Karl awoke. A hard floor made waking early easy. Cracking open the front door, he saw that the snow had stopped.

"Wake up, Tony. The storm is over and we got to get going." Hearing a shuffle behind him, Karl turned. The old man was walking to the stove with an armload of wood.

"Have your coffee ready shortly."

Stoking up the ashes and adding some wood, the poorly-fit sections of the stove began to smoke. Soon, the fire would start and create a draft, sending the smoke up the chimney. He walked over to a pail and, using the dipper to break the thin sheet of ice, he added water to the pot. Placing it onto the stove, he dumped some fresh coffee to mix with the old.

Tony volunteered to get the horses ready. He stepped out of the door. Karl could hear the snow crunching under his feet as Tony walked around the building.

The old man had the bearskin down from the wall. He folded it into a neat bundle.

"Make you bacon and fried bread for breakfast if you want. Just a dollar."

The gold coin must be used up, Karl thought. "Sure, that would be fine. It includes coffee right?"

Another toothless grin from the old man. "Sure does."

After another surprisingly good meal, other than the coffee, Karl and Tony were in the saddle and off. Karl had the bearskin securely tied onto the back of his saddle.

They made good time. The snow was knee-deep on the animals. The horses that they had were long legged and had no trouble. They made over their 60 mile goal. There was a full moon and they were able to keep riding until almost midnight.

In the crisp night air, they rubbed the horses down and put blankets over them. The temperature was well below freezing and the horses were warm from the fast pace. Nose bags with oats were put on the horses. Karl built a small fire for coffee. Tony warmed a biscuit near the fire while waiting for the coffee. He took some cheese out of his inside coat pocket, sliced a piece and put it onto his warm biscuit. Smiling, Tony then made one for Karl.

They awoke the next morning with two inches of fresh snow covering their blankets. Shaking the snow off and slipping their stiff, frozen boots on, a pot of coffee was brewed for breakfast. Tony sat on a log wrapped in the deerskin coat that Ruth had made him. Karl felt a twinge of envy. It looked much warmer than his army coat.

Another hard day's riding brought them to the banks of the Turkey River. Karl and Tony could see the snow-covered yard. Karl noticed that the porch was not shoveled and that there was no smoke coming from the chimney.

Wading the horses across the river, they rode up into the yard. Dismounting, Tony walked toward the porch. The place felt strange and lifeless. He wondered if this was what they meant about not being able to go back. The sound of jingling harnesses caught their attention as a large black horse came around the house, pulling a buggy. Tate and Jacob Wolfe stepped down from the buggy.

"Welcome home, boys. Did you have a nice trip?" Tate sneered.

Karl walked toward the Wolfe brothers. "We are here to pay off the note."

Tate waved him away with his hand. "Too late, boys. The deal is done."

"I believe the note is due the last day of November. It is only the 29th," Karl said clearly.

"Your mother saw no way of paying and had not heard from you. She left the house two days ago," Tate replied. He was really enjoying this.

"Leaving the house does not make it yours. Being gone for two days means nothing. You cannot register the deed until December 1st, and that is only if not paid."

Tate was getting angry. He was already building a warehouse on the site in his mind. Jacob stepped forward with fist clenched.

"I must warn you, I have a money belt filled with gold on. You don't want to break another wrist, do you?" Karl coldly asked.

Jacob hesitated and stepped back. Tate snorted, "You young pups are out of your class going against us. I'll have you both in jail for trespassing."

Karl decided to take another tack. It was one he was not proud of, but he was mad clear through.

"Mr. Wolfe, you are not talking to your boys now. James did his best to stop us at the direction of you and Josh. He died bravely fighting off Comanches, but would not have died except for your orders." Karl saw Tate stiffen at the name of his son

James. "Due to your orders to Josh, he died trying to rob and kill us before we could come back with the gold."

Karl knew that Tate Wolfe did not know about Josh. He saw pure shock sweep across Tate Wolfe's face. Karl was immediately sorry that he had told him about his son's death in such a way.

Karl watched as Tate moved his hand toward his revolver.

"If your hand touches the grip of your gun, I will put a knife in your chest before you can clear leather," Tony warned.

Tate had heard these words before from a ragged man who had walked out of the river oh-so-many years ago. The man had married the woman who should have been his.

Tate Wolfe felt his knees going weak and stumbled back against the carriage. Jacob grabbed his brother to help support him.

Jacob had tears in his eyes. "Both sons dead? What will my brother do now? Who will carry on his work?" Slowly, Jacob helped Tate into the carriage.

Looking at Karl, Jacob said, "Meet me at the bank in an hour with the money. We will take care of the note today."

Karl could see that Tate Wolfe was a crushed man. He had run a gamble with his sons as pawns, and he had lost. He had lost the opportunity to pass his legacy down to his own flesh and blood.

The Wolfe's carriage pulled around the end of the house. Karl and Tony walked to the porch.

"Nice job with father's words, Tony," Karl said.

"The opportunity only comes once in a lifetime, Karl." Tony jumped up on the porch and opened the door for his brother.

The first thing that Karl wanted to do was warm up the house. "Tony, start a fire in the stove. We got to bring this home back to life. I'll put our horses in the barn."

As he led the horse into the double doors of the building, the warm, moist air, pungent with the smells of the animals, hit him. Memories of running from the house on cold mornings and looking forward to the warmth of the barn while feeding the stock flooded back. On the coldest days he would hug the cows, to share their body heat.

He pulled off the gear and rubbed down the horses before putting them into the box stalls. The last thing that he wanted was the major to find the animals ill from being put up wet. After giving them some grain, he pitched hay to all of the stock.

Leaving the saddle bags in the barn, Karl walked toward the house, happy to see the smoke rising from the chimney. They had been gone for over six months and he hadn't realized how important being home was.

Kicking the snow off his boots, Karl walked into the house. The warmth of the stove, the smell of the burning wood, and coffee that Tony had going were comforting. The only thing missing was the smell of cookies or bread baking.

The cupboards were mostly empty. It was evident that their mother hadn't expected them to get back in time, if ever.

While drinking the strong coffee, Tony said, "I keep expecting to see our father walk in the door."

Both looked toward the fireplace, where their father had laid in his coffin. While it now seemed like long ago, the pain of the loss flood over both of the boys. Karl held up his cup. "To our father. May he be watching over us in heaven." Tony touched his cup to Karl's and they both drank.

Sitting for moment in silence, Karl said, "We best get to the bank and then see if mother and Jenny are at the Keller's."

They added more wood to the stove before leaving. The snow crunched under their boots as they walked toward the bank. They found the shades down and the door locked. Grasping the knob, Karl shook it and then pounded on the door.

"If you and Blevins are in there, Jacob, you best open this door!" he shouted.

Kicking the bottom of the door, he turned to Tony. "Damn that man!" Karl bristled. "If he tries to hide so we can't pay the note, I'll . . ."

"Karl!" Tony cautioned him. "The whole town can hear you. Blevins may have closed the bank for personal reasons. We'll just go over to Wolfe's place and see him there."

Jacob Wolfe lived in a stately home on the north end of Elkader. The boys were anxious to let their mother know that they were back. But if she was at the Keller's, their house was on the south end of town. Right now they were both driven to get their hands on the note.

The two brothers walked passed the mercantile. George Walters, the owner, was standing outside the door. "What's all the noise?" Seeing the boys, he said, "Oh, you're back."

"Yes, we're back," Karl replied, brushing by the man.

"Now, Karl," Tony hissed. "We got to live with these people. We don't know that Jacob didn't also find the bank closed. We got plenty of time to be mad if we find out he's trying to dodge us."

The buggy with the black horse was standing in front of the house. They climbed onto the freshly shoveled porch and knocked on the door. Tony remembered playing on this porch when his friend was visiting his uncle. He shook his head and whispered, "Josh."

The door was opened by a white-haired woman. Her eyes were red from crying. "Come in please," she said. "Jacob is expecting you."

Leading them to the dining room, she hurried away. Jacob and the banker, Paul Blevins, sat drinking tea. Karl didn't see Tate anywhere.

Clearing his throat, Jacob said, "Have a seat. Nellie will bring you some tea."

In front of him he had the note. He pushed it to Karl, "I have already signed off it. I trust you have the money. You can go with Paul to the bank and deposit it in my account."

Feeling uncomfortable, Karl apologized. "I was wrong telling Tate about Josh the way I did."

Jacob's wife, Nellie, came into the room with a tray holding a tea pot and two cups with saucers. Paul Blevins moved the sugar and cream toward the boys.

"I didn't know about what my brother had asked the boys to do," the man explained. "I won't say that I didn't hope you would fail, but not that way."

The tea was hot and it took forever to drink it. Karl and Tony wanted nothing more than to be out of that house. Finally finished, Tony said, "Mr. Blevins, if we could go to the bank now."

Jacob escorted the banker and the brothers to the door. Before Karl stepped out, he said, "Someday I would like to know more about what happened on the drive and where Tate's sons are buried."

As Jacob walked away, he added, "And were the gold was."

Karl clutched the note in his gloved hand as they entered the bank. Taking a seat behind the teller's windows, he took some of the gold out of the money belt. The banker brought his scale over and, after satisfying himself that the gold was pure, he weighed out the amount needed to pay the note.

"There in an additional fee for discharging the note," the banker said. "You are responsible for it."

At last the business of the note was complete. Karl put all of the paperwork into the money belt and thanked the banker.

"I imagine you or your mother will be depositing the rest of the gold with the bank," Mr. Blevins said, finally smiling.

"We will, but right now we have to see our mother," Tony answered.

"I believe she is at the Keller's," the banker told them.

Thanking him again, they hurried out of the bank and headed south of town. Passing the telegraph office, Tony reminded Karl, "We got to send a message to the family of Tim Cross. They should know what happened to him."

Putting it off until later, they arrived at the Keller's place. Karl knocked on the door and they waited impatiently. Mrs. Keller opened it and a look of surprise crossed her face.

Karl and Tony saw their mother standing in the kitchen. Mrs. August's boys ran across the room and hugged their mother as she began to cry.

"Everything is alright, mother," Karl whispered.

* * *

Within an hour Joan August and her children were headed back home. She was determined to be back in her home on the Turkey River before the sun set. While Joan and Jenny picked up supplies from the mercantile, the brothers sent the telegram to the Cross family. Coming out, they saw that the ladies had two large bags waiting for them.

While they walked toward the house, Joan told Tony, "Tell me about Ruth. Your letter said you'll be a father."

Blushing he said, "Yes, I will. I can't wait for you to meet her. Major Thomas is bringing the ladies and should be here in less than a week."

"Where is Poco staying?" Karl asked.

"He is such a nice man," Joan said. "I tried to get him to stay at the Keller's with Jenny and me, but he insisted on staying at the hotel."

Arriving at the house, Karl wished that he and Tony had taken a minute to shovel the porch off. The warmth as they stepped into the house made up for it. The ladies went to put the groceries away while Tony hauled in some wood and Karl shoveled off the porch.

Joan came to the door and looked at her son shoveling. "You need to warm the sauna. You and your brother are in desperate need of a bath and shave."

Albert came by in time to help with the wood hauling. While their supper was cooking, the family sat around the fireplace and drank warm cider. Albert wanted to know every detail of the search for gold.

After the meal was over, Karl and Tony sat in the sauna, throwing water onto the hot rocks. Karl ran his fingers over the scars of the wounds that he had received. They would be something to remind him of how lucky he had been.

"What are we going to tell Jacob about Josh's burial?" Tony asked his brother.

Karl tossed another dipper of water onto the rocks. Plumbs of steam filled the small room. "I will tell him that Josh rests near a river, north of Fort Dakota."

After their sauna, the brothers hurried through the winter night back to the house, their hair freezing in the frigid cold.

Until late in the evening the brothers and Albert told stories of the cattle drive. Many of the more dangerous details were left out, making the trip a much more enjoyable adventure. None of the men mentioned Haat. That would be left for later.

Plans were made by Karl and Tony to find Poco the next morning, while Jenny and her mother talked of plans for a triple wedding.

Tired from a long day, the younger August children went to their beds. Karl and his mother sat at the kitchen table. He got up and went to his coat hanging on a peg near the door. Removing the ledger from the pocket, he placed it in front of Joan.

Taking his seat next to her, he said, "I want to thank you for letting us take this on our trip. We found reading the notes father had written helped us get over his loss."

Joan held it close, touching her lips to it. "This ledger was as important to your father's survival as the Good Knife. Writing in it gave him a purpose to get through each day."

Squirming in his chair, Karl knew that it was time to tell his mother about Haat. Working to get his nerve up, he took their cups and refilled them with coffee. His mother watched him.

"You look troubled, son," she said softly.

"Mother, you have read the ledger, right?" he asked.

"Yes, I have. Many times," she replied. "You have heard the stories about your father having the gold stolen after he got here. That was the first time. The ledger was left in the jail while he went with the sheriff to catch those that took it. I found it and read through it. As tattered as your father was when I first saw him, I was attracted to the man in rags. Reading about what he had survived made me fall in love with him."

"Do you recall the part about saving Nina?" he asked.

His mother thought back for a moment. "Yes. He saved her from a wild cat."

"Tony and I met her son on our trip," he told her.

"You did?" she asked, surprised. "How did you find out it was her son?"

Karl traced the indention on the cover of the ledger. "He was wearing something around his neck that his mother had given him with the same shape and holes for the rivets as is on the ledger."

Confused, she said, "I don't understand."

Taking a deep breath, Karl told her of the meeting when driving the horses and Haat saying that his father's name was "Auugus, and had hair of gold."

"His mother had told him the same stories about being attacked by the cat as father wrote in his ledger. He is our brother," Karl explained.

The confused look on Joan's face slowly changed to a smile. "I must meet them some day."

"You will, mother. I'm sure you will," Karl said, taking her hands in his.

With tears coming to her eyes, she said, "And then there's Ruth, the baby, and Karen. My goodness, the family is growing so fast."

His own eyes beginning to smart, Karl said, "You'll love Ruth and Karen. They are pure gold."

MORE GOLD

I hope you enjoyed reading *Search For Oli's Gold* as much as I enjoyed writing it. You can continue following the gold with *Return To Oli's Gold*. My goal is to continue to provide quality books for your enjoyment. I would appreciate you taking the time to post a positive review. You can do so by going to the books Amazon page. Scroll down to the button saying "Write a customer review", click it and enter your comments.

Watch for future books as they become available. Your support will be the fuel to motivate my writing.

Best wishes and good reading.

Jim

OTHER BOOKS BY THE AUTHOR

Oli's Gold: Book One

Search For Oli's Gold: Book Two

Return To Oli's Gold: Book Three

To Be A Mountain Man

Trouble On The Kansas Plain

Frontier Justice

Return Of The Mountain Man

The Tall Man